THE ALICE

Celebrating
30 Years of Publishing
in India

THE ALICE PROJECT

SATWIK GADE

HarperCollins *Publishers* India

First published in India by HarperCollins *Publishers* 2023
4th Floor, Tower A, Building No. 10, Phase II, DLF Cyber City,
Gurugram, Haryana – 122002
www.harpercollins.co.in

2 4 6 8 10 9 7 5 3 1

P-ISBN: 978-93-5629-506-3
E-ISBN: 978-93-5629-507-0

Typeset in 11.5/15.7 Minion Pro at
Manipal Technologies Limited, Manipal

Printed and bound at
Thomson Press (India) Ltd

For my parents

BOOK I

Winter

1

While descending a mountain, your heavy head leans over to look down at what's beneath. It is bound to feel the pull of gravity. The scene shifts to your centre of gravity. The little ogre that lives inside your belly button comes out of his cave and, deftly pulling itself up using your coiled body hair and supple flesh, climbs all the way up to your head and whacks you on the cranium with its club. You fall. You tumble and you tumble and you tumble. Then there is the edge and then the fall. The fall is long, but you are bound to find out it's a dream and then the fall eases before you land on the mattress, abdomen squeezed in.

Alice felt his shoulder blades first. And then his heels. He struggled for a while with his sheets before wrenching them out from underneath his body. He yawned, stretched and scratched himself, much like a cat, before he finally sat up. He reached for his mobile which was next to his pillow and pressed the button on the top left. 'The time is 9.30 a.m.' A robot's impression of a female voice. Twisting himself hip upwards, he tried to look around the room. Everything was still blurry. The pixelated form of Bakchod, his roommate, with his back to the wall, typing away at his laptop, reminded Alice that he was in his own room. His dreams tended to disorientate him.

He felt around under his pillow and found the morning cigarette. He smoothed it out as much as he could, lit its crumpled tip with some difficulty, and blew out rich smoke straight at Bakchod hoping to annoy him. Glaring at Alice, Bakchod continued to bang away at his laptop, now with increased vigour. Alice took a deep breath and shook his head. An involuntary shiver broke at his neck and ran all the way down to the base of his spine. That woke him up. His vision was getting better too.

'Order tea?' he asked Bakchod in a kind of early morning growl-hiss.

'No.'

'Tea! Now!' Growl-gasp-cough-hiss.

'Order it yourself. I've got work.'

'No voice.' And he made a sad face. Bakchod grumbled something, partially inaudible, about cigarettes and a Lancer before ordering four cups of chai and two buns deep fried in lard. 'Don't look so grumpy on a lovely Saturday, Bakchod. Don't you think it's finally cold enough for a bonfire party? Play some fiery patriotic songs from Bhagat Singh or something, no. Warm up the cockles.'

Bakchod, virtually untranslatable, is roughly talk-fucker. One who fucks you with his talk. One who talks like a fuck.

One who fucks any talk. One whose talk makes you feel fucked. And so on. He had earned this title very early in his first semester as he talk-fucked his way through many a ragging session until the seniors baptized and turned him into a minor college celebrity for a while. With time, fame faded, but the name stuck.

Bakchod physically abused a few more keys on the laptop and squinted at the screen. 'Too early for Bhagat, man. Let's play some soothing devotional songs. I'm in a mood for some Meera Bai!' Then, looking at Alice, he said, 'Don't forget to fold the sheets before you go to the loo!' Alice yawned again and an aimless mosquito wandered into his mouth. He coughed the mosquito out on to the sheets along with some phlegm.

Bakchod and Alice had been living in that room since the fourth year of college. It was a fairly neat twelve-by-twelve, with an attached bathroom; originally meant to be a part of the servant quarters. It had a couple of windows with a grill that was not screwed in properly and therefore detachable. The safety of the items in the room, Bakchod's laptop included, depended on nobody realizing that the grill was detachable. They had a single key that was always with Bakchod. Thanks to the detachable grill, they never got a duplicate made. The bathroom was tiny but very fancy, with a shower, western commode and a French jet-thingy that shot streams of water directly up one's asshole.

When the chai arrived, the two of them went to the terrace to enjoy hot tea in the winter sun. The urchin had lingered around for a tip. Bakchod rotated his index finger while jerking his wrist and shooed him off.

A resident of the east coast for the first seventeen years of his life, Alice had never experienced, first hand, a seasonal change of any sort unless one counted a slight dip in temperature around Christmas and a more than slight rise in it during the holidays. It is for that reason that his eighteenth birthday had been one of the best, because he got to wear, for the first time, a jacket, a muffler and a winter hat, valiantly ignoring his brain, which kept telling him he looked like the bearded crook from *Home Alone*. It was primarily because of this that he came to love the Delhi winters and consequently the winter sun, which was, to quote Upamanyu Chatterjee, 'rare, slim, comforting and therefore, vaguely erotic.'

~

On weekends, Alice and Bakchod lunched with their friends who lived on the other side of the colony. Nitin and Iyengar (Padmavathi Balakrishnan, referred to by Alice and Bakchod only by her caste name) had been their classmates and closest friends during college and had, despite Alice's protests and warnings of impending doom, started dating a couple of years earlier. 'Of course you two are happy now,' Alice told them as often as he could. 'But soon you'll have a bitter breakup and expect me to choose. Then, and I kid you not when I say this, I'll fart in your faces and make new friends!'

On the way down from their room, Alice and Bakchod were intercepted by the landlord's wife (rumoured to be his second, the one for whom he had had the first one killed) and invited inside the house. She was a plump lady with small, shrewd eyes and a fat nose. If this is how the one he fell in love with looks, chuckled Alice's brain, I shudder to think how dreadful the first one must have looked! The landlord had a real estate agency in the locality that was a front for various shady businesses; it was run by his two sons. Being the retired ganglord of the area, he had many illegal flats around the locality which he very graciously rented out to students at higher prices for the added safety of being under his wing. Everyone who knew him was terrified of him, including and especially, his two sons, so much so, that they put aside their property disputes and ran the agency amicably. The old man was rather fond of Bakchod and had rented his own servant quarters out to him. Alice was only a co-beneficiary and so was never spoken to directly on matters of lodging and rent.

'Why are you sitting in the living room? Come and sit here,' said the landlord in between letting out a jack-hammer belch indicating his approval of the food.

'At the dining table? It's okay. We are quite comfortable here,' said Alice hurriedly.

'Arrey yaar, there's something important I need to discuss with you people.' He frowned at Alice, presumably for speaking out of turn.

He was like an iceberg behind the dining table, showing only his soft face, his sad eyes and a portion of his chest. Unlike the upper body that appeared to be like one belonging to a normal human being, his lower portion was swollen like a bottle gourd. Not maybe as fat as Whopping Walter Hudson from the CBSE textbook, but still, extremely fat for someone who moved around a lot. The first time Alice saw him standing, he was amazed at the girth of his lower body; especially, the buttocks. They seemed to be on the verge of a mitotic phase of separation from his body. If I sleep the way I sleep in winters, Alice remembered thinking to himself, I could fit snugly on one butt cheek.

They had been called there to discuss an increase in rent. Another thunderous belch. 'I think you should increase the rent by at least twelve per cent from the next month.' Alice was about to nod his assent; they had been staying there for over a year, but Bakchod kicked him under the table and simpered, 'Uncle-ji, why don't you just kill us instead?' Then a brave smile and 'We just don't have that kind of money. We are already paying you the maximum we can.' He used the English word 'maximum' like an efficient sales executive who knew how to drop buzzwords and also, when to drop them.

'You know I love you like my own son, in fact much more than those two imbeciles, but the prices are increasing everywhere. I swear! You people are staying here for half the market price.'

'Please, we cannot pay more than a six per cent increase. Our starting salaries are shamefully bad. And I don't even want to talk about the recession,' Bakchod said and proceeded to do exactly that.

Some pleasant haggling, pleading and sycophancy ensued. After the central government and state government, Lehman Brothers and Wall Street were also duly apportioned blame. Bakchod did all the talking. Alice made some incoherent noises whenever he was asked his opinion by either of them, all the while angry with Bakchod for talking shit when they could easily afford the difference. Finally: 'Oh god! I can't believe I'm agreeing to this. *Theek hai*, six per cent from next month.'

'Thanks, uncle-ji. What would we do without you? Achcha, we are getting late for lunch, we'll take your leave now.'

As they were leaving, the landlord smiled at Alice and said, 'Your friend is one persuasive motherfucker!' Bakchod grinned shyly and walked away with Alice in his wake.

~

Nitin and Iyengar lived in the gali where dogs slept on nights they decided to die. The gali was noisy during the day but deathly silent at night. At least two times Alice had seen dogs humping in the afternoon on the same day that a dog died in the night. Seeing karmic cycles play out in a dusty fly-ridden nook of the colony was unsettling but Alice felt it also was somehow profound.

Lunch this weekend was lavish. Nitin cooked good home food. Iyengar was hopeless in the kitchen and was quite proud of the fact, in a women's emancipation kind of way. All the food was cooked in homemade ghee that had come from Nitin's ancestral village last month. They all had an ancestral village from where periodically emerged mangoes, pickles, dairy products and relatives, in the order of how welcome they were. Nitin's village was the closest and he had a grandmother still in it, while the others didn't even have one who was alive. His grandmother owned a big, black and beautiful buffalo whose yield produced ghee that tasted like heaven. Its heavenly taste was partly the reason why Alice and Bakchod had passionately expressed shock when they had found out that the buffalo didn't have a name.

'What do you mean it doesn't have a name?'

'It just doesn't, that's all.'

'Why doesn't it have a name?'

'We have only one buffalo.'

'You only have one penis but she named it!' Bakchod had said angrily while pointing at Iyengar. Iyengar had lunged and bit his finger so hard his skin broke and she drew blood. Nitin later told Alice, 'You know before she got all soft and started apologizing to him, that one second where she was glaring at him with his blood on her face? Man! That's the most turned on I have ever been.'

'Me too!' Alice wanted to say but didn't.

Presently, Bakchod poured a lot of ghee on his plate and proceeded to attack the food. The others watched in silent amazement as he gobbled up twice his share of food and announced that they absolutely must have 'the lovely brownie and ice cream at this small bakery I discovered behind the gurdwara. The brownie is so tasty, it's not even funny!' That was his favourite expression. According to him, upon reaching the superlative of their own adjective, things ceased to be humorous, for unexplained reasons.

The bakery was called—no prizes for guessing—Cakes and Bakes. On their way there, Alice realized that there was a Cakes and Bakes in every one of the seven cities that he had lived in. Maybe people in general were like that, placing functionality over novelty. Maybe it was enough for many that their lone buffalo was just referred to as 'bhains'. Only a minority, he decided, were probably like Bakchod. They would sit up at night thinking up unique names for things they owned. It was because of this whimsical nature of Bakchod that Alice had become friends with him when several others found him incredibly annoying. There were times when he, like everyone else, hated Bakchod for his endless reserve of energy that was used, more often than not, to play pranks and talk copious quantities of bullshit. Nevertheless, very often, he would grudgingly admire Bakchod's hedonism, his sheer lust for life.

Over brownie and ice cream (tasty as promised), Nitin announced that he had been offered a job as a junior fashion designer in Bangalore. 'I don't know if I'll be taking it up, but the offer is really good. Anyway, I don't have to decide for another week or so. I'm just telling you guys now so you can't complain later.' Bakchod dropped his spoon in surprise, but immediately slapped Nitin on the back and said, 'Congrats, fucker! Migrating to greener pastures. Speaking of greener pastures, Iyengar, do you know chicks in Bangalore are super-hot?' Iyengar laughed and asked Bakchod to fuck off but there was something weird about her laugh. Alice looked at his brownie, letting the news sink in. Nitin and he had been the best of friends since the beginning of college. Nitin was always the friend, philosopher and guide type of person whom you could count on for sober advice. The one you looked up to. Realizing he had been quiet for a few seconds too long, he quickly grinned and joined Bakchod, 'Long distance is going to be a bitch. I told you guys not to start dating!'

~

Saturday nights were times of unhindered fantasizing and endless laziness. Whisky-soda in the warmth of a small bonfire. Alice and Bakchod were looking through broken pieces of furniture that the neighbours had discarded so that they could be used as firewood. The bonfire would be on the terrace of their four-storeyed building. The apartment was just a couple of streets away from college. It was very easy to locate because it stood opposite a very important landmark—Amitabh Bachchan's house. Legend has it that Amitabh Bachchan had bought the house following the success of *Deewar*. Although he had never actually lived there, he had visited the house twice in the last four years preventing Alice and Bakchod from getting to their college on time on both occasions.

They found a sufficient amount of wood and managed to break it into smaller pieces. Armed with a jacket and a muffler, Alice made his way to the terrace. By 8.30 p.m., he had a decent fire going. He sat on a flat stone poking at the fire lazily with a broken golf club—also a discarded piece previously owned by the generous-by-default neighbours— when Iyengar arrived. Unexpectedly, she brought along her new colleague-friend whom no one had met before. A few days later, Alice told Nitin that he had fallen for Snigdha the moment he had set eyes on her. This was, of course, a stupendous lie. When they were introduced, 'Alice. Snigdha. Snigdha. Alice.', he thought she was rather plain looking and silently cursed Iyengar for not making friends with hotter girls. If her friend were any hotter, Mr Donkey Brains, you wouldn't have a chance in hell with her, his brain pointed out. She looks decent and seems smart, so keep an open mind, it advised.

'Alice! That's your name?' She had a husky voice.

'That's what they call me,' he said, with what he hoped was a charming smile. 'You'll get used to it soon enough.'

They sat by the fire, chatting about random things, while Iyengar left to fetch Nitin and Bakchod. He found out she used to work for an organization that did stuff like searching for new species of animals while roaming about in dense rainforests. She was getting involved in a tiger conservation project and would soon be travelling all over India. He was very impressed by and slightly envious of her for pursuing so noble a profession. Inevitably she asked him what he did. He smiled stupidly. 'I am a designer. I brand things. I am the reason things cost much more than they need to.'

'Also the reason I am buying things I don't need?'

'Yes, and also the reason everything looks strangely similar these days. Like a copy of a copy of a copy.' Snigdha smiled in acknowledgement of the reference and Alice smiled back, happy that she got the reference. 'But I don't hate my job. Well, I do hate it in the sense that, what's to like in a job, but other than that I am okay with it. It's certainly not something I can be passionate about, but...'

'Why not?'

'Well, when you achieve something—I don't know— science expands or species are saved. When I do my job, one of my boss's rich friends gets more clients at his restaurant.'

'No, but you see...' then she looked down slowly with a sheepish smile and said, 'I don't know what to say. When you put it that way, it does sound pretty bad, but you know, hey, you brand a company, they make a lot of money. They think, okay, as part of our CSR drive let's pump a lot of money into, say ... saving tigers! Huh? That would be cool.

That could happen. The cause-and-effect chain is pretty complex, right?'

'Thanks. I don't buy any of what you are saying, but good effort and might I say it was delivered with panache!'

She laughed. It was like a toddler splashing about in a bathtub.

Alice smiled and let his gaze linger on her a little too long. Breaking out of it, he said, 'What does saving tigers entail, by the way? I mean everyone knows we need to save tigers but … you know…'

'Wow!' she exclaimed and exhaled dramatically, 'I don't know where to start, but I could go on and on. I mean there is no one way, really. Basically, it is textbook stuff. Like, you need to involve local populations in intelligently planned conservation programmes. Or, you need really driven and passionate forest rangers to implement these programmes.'

'What about poaching? I've seen Captain Planet.'

'Ah, nice to meet a fellow planeteer!' They laughed. 'Yeah, poaching is a huge problem, but again it really comes down to engaging the local populations, so you always have intelligence on poaching activities in the area.'

'And this is not happening?'

'Sure, in many places to some extent and to a great extent in some places, but not nearly enough. See, you can at least get a stranglehold on politicians through dharnas or during the elections, but how do you fight bureaucratic apathy? The process is slow and requires a great deal of patience and reading a lot of boring books and writing letters. But this is all theory and second-hand information I've picked up from colleagues. I'll really know once I...'

Iyengar, Nitin and Bakchod came in with the booze. More introductions were followed by the pouring of whisky, soda and water. 'To new friends,' said Snigdha and they all bottoms upped the first drink as was their custom. While finishing off the first bottle, they talked, politely and cautiously at first, and then when the whisky hit them, loudly and exuberantly.

Since it was the first bonfire of the season, they decided to keep it 'family only' and hadn't invited any of their usual gang. So Alice was saved the trouble of worrying about other guys talking to Snigdha. Bakchod got a call from his girlfriend, who was working in Mumbai, asking him to log on to Skype. He grumbled perfunctorily, downed the contents of his glass in one gulp and left.

The terrace was not meant to be a recreational area at all. It was merely a storage area for the water tanks and hence had no proper walls. Parts of the locality were visible and the four of them languidly watched people walking hurriedly down the road and security guards gathering around small fires they had made for themselves. Since they could see several streets from up there, each time a bunch of stray dogs fought, it felt like they were watching a helicopter camera-chase sequence, being able to follow the dogs across many a lane. By the end of around four fights, with Snigdha explaining to him the territorial instincts of animals, Alice felt he had managed to gain a rough idea of each gang's territory.

'Man,' said Alice to Snigdha wistfully, since he was past the complete contentment stage of his drunkenness, 'I really wish I were one of those dogs you know. I'd have my own gang, like Shah Rukh Khan in *Josh*. I'd have this ... this little dark patch of fur around my head and eyes to signify the band and goggles. I'd bark badass songs at the Bicchhoo gang down the street.'

'We're talking about gangs and your ultimate fantasy situation is *Josh*?' laughed Snigdha.

Iyengar, too, laughed. 'We found a school notebook of his that had "Eagles vs Bicchhoo" scribbled in all the margins and end pages.'

Grinning sheepishly, Alice said, 'The heart wants what it wants. And Priya Gill was way ahead of her time.'

The topic turned to Nitin's new job and Iyengar suddenly grew extremely interested in the small print on the whisky bottle. All of a sudden, the air came to bear the weight of an unspoken anxiety. However, Snigdha, quite oblivious of it, asked questions with much enthusiasm and Nitin answered in single sentences and small phrases. Alice looked up; the sky above was sprinkled with a few stars here and there. He finished the rest of his glass in a single gulp and poured himself another one.

Bakchod came back some time later looking happy and generally loved. The first bottle was nearly finished. He downed the rest in a go and helped them get back to talking shit. The second bottle went down amidst a psychedelic daze of stories, jokes and Bakchod's confessions of eternal love for them. With the second bottle down, Alice did not care any more that Snigdha was there, or that it was well past midnight in a residential neighbourhood, and joined Bakchod in dancing to Govinda songs. Nitin tried to stop them but he was too drunk to try very hard. When Iyengar fell asleep with her head on Nitin's lap, Alice and Bakchod took advantage of Nitin's immobility by poking and tickling him while they danced. Soon the singing turned to shrieking and the choice of songs got more rustic, in turn exciting them into shrieking even louder. Snigdha seemed to enjoy herself and clapped vigorously in an effort to match the rhythm of their inebriated howls but failed horribly.

As they were singing the second stanza of 'Sarkailo khatiya', they heard a police siren at a distance. Surprisingly, Iyengar was the first to hear it in her sleep. She woke up mumbling, 'Pulees, pulees.' Bakchod's eyes widened in excitement, and he screeched, 'Pandoooo log! Hahahaha! Pandooo!' Alice soon caught on, grabbed the bucket of sand they always kept on the terrace and put the fire out. Bakchod continued to shout 'Pandoo! Pandoo!' until Nitin slapped him across the face and caught him by the collar, threatening dire consequences if he didn't shut up. The sound of the siren got louder and louder until they could hear the sound of the engine too and then both sounds abruptly stopped. The five of them hurried downstairs to the room. They shoved Bakchod into the loo, and he promptly started to hurl into the commode. Alice and Snigdha crouched in the darkest corner and trembled silently as Nitin switched off all the lights, locked the room from the outside, detached the grill, jumped in, reattached the grill and closed the window in under two minutes. Respect, said Alice's brain gravely. Iyengar went into the loo to try and gag Bakchod who had stopped retching but was now sobbing and sniffing, making sounds that carried.

As the sound of footsteps became audible, Bakchod's sobs subsided, and Nitin joined Alice and Snigdha in the corner. The footsteps got louder and louder and stopped right outside the door. The voices outside seemed eerily close to Alice, who covered his mouth with his palms not even daring to breathe. He was very drunk and, in his crouched position, seemed to be in danger of falling on to Bakchod's laptop, which was right behind him. To make matters worse, his left hand inadvertently kept brushing against the side of Snigdha's breast and every time that happened, his heart exploded so loudly he was surprised the police couldn't hear it. Snigdha was swaying quite a lot, unable to balance herself on her heels. She grabbed Nitin's shoulder for support, making him almost cry out in surprise. Iyengar was still in the loo with Bakchod. Judging from the pin-drop silence, Bakchod had either passed out or Iyengar had killed him, thought Alice. Either was fine with him.

The police were talking amongst themselves now.

'This fucking door is locked! And that house has an old couple living in it. So which eunuch's cunt was making all that noise?' a gruff voice enquired.

'Sir, somebody was having a bonfire here.' A distant servile voice. Some more footsteps. More chatter.

'Why did all you cunts run up the same flight of stairs? Maybe they went down the other flight of stairs. Go down and see.' Some more footsteps, some more chatter. Then silence for a while.

'Sir, whoever it was, they won't dare come back. So maybe we can leave?' the servile voice enquired with much hesitation. A curt 'hmm' and more footsteps.

The guy with the gruff voice hung around for some more time, muttering obscenities, and then walked away. Ten minutes later, Alice heard the sound of the jeep's engine spring to life and then get distinctly less audible before fading away altogether. Without turning the lights on or even talking, Snigdha walked up to Bakchod's mattress, quietly lay down and covered herself with a blanket. A few seconds later, the bathroom door creaked open apprehensively as Iyengar staggered out and collapsed next to Snigdha. Maybe she did kill Bakchod, Alice thought, but his brain pointed out to him that there were two girls under one blanket. Giggling drunkenly, he looked around for Nitin and found him spreading out Alice's sleeping bag next to the mattress. He wanted to say, your girlfriend is a lesbo, but he suddenly realized Bakchod was still in the loo.

Such opportunities arise very rarely, his brain pointed out to him. Carpe diem, good sir!

'Get up, asshole. Bakchod has passed out in the loo. Probably in his own puke,' whispered Alice, shaking Nitin by the shoulder.

'Listen, I don't have the energy to clean him up now. We'll see what we can do tomorrow,' replied Nitin in a hushed baritone.

'No, you bloody uncle! Fetch Iyengar's iPhone! We need to take photos!'

They found Iyengar's phone in her handbag and opened the bathroom door. Bakchod lay there sprawled on the floor, snoring lightly with one hand still holding the toilet seat. A trickle of vomit escaped from the side of his mouth and found its way down his neck. Making as little noise as possible, Nitin and Alice took photos of Bakchod at all possible angles. Even their carrying whispers did not wake Bakchod up. Of all the photos, the best one was the final signature photograph. Alice, flashing a peace sign and a wide smile sitting next to the passed-out Bakchod and Nitin, his head appearing sideways in the frame, making a devil's horn sign. He had clicked the photo by turning the phone around with his other hand. A year later, they would start referring to it as a selfie.

2

Where do the kulfiwalas go during the winters?

Walking down the road that led to the bus stop, Alice was trying to simultaneously avoid auto drivers (most of whom turn psychopathic through years of sustained road rage and class oppression), enervated stray dogs catching a nap, all manners of oral and rectal excrements, and disenfranchised youth looking to pick a fight. Having lived in the city for the last four years, all this had become second nature to him to the extent that his mind wandered towards the kulfiwalas, made conspicuous by the absence of tinkling bells and cries advertising their wares.

'The kulfiwalas are probably hibernating,' said Javed, in a weak attempt at humour, when Alice called in the morning to invite himself over. And thus, while getting ready and packing, he texted half-assed excuses to his boss about why he wouldn't be able to make it to office.

Behind the college, next to the enormous jungle of concrete crap that was the metro construction, stood the Yusuf Sarai bus stop. The perennially full bus arrived after a fifteen-minute wait, wobbling, slightly leaning to the right, with a mob emerging from its doors like a flower bouquet.

Alice fought his way into the bus and allowed himself to be squeezed through to a spot where his foot found itself under a woman's grocery bag and his face was shoved into the armpit of a well-built Sardar. He loved winters for the fact that people weren't sweaty and also accumulated pheromones from not bathing. This man seemed to have even slapped some aftershave on his pits. The pheromones and musk made for a heady mix.

When the Sardar and some others got off at one of the stops, Alice's eyes began to rove unconsciously. Before long he spotted a cleavage. He shuffled nonchalantly and got a better vantage point. I hope you realize what you are doing is utterly disgusting, his brain spat. The next five minutes were spent trying not to stare at the cleavage which was getting more and more prominent at every speed bump owing to the fact that the woman seemed to be wearing a kameez two sizes too big for her. Social etiquette and youthful depravity battled each other. Finally, he decided to distract himself by composing a letter to the Transport Corporation stating that men must sit and women stand so as to preserve the delicate moral fabric of the Indian society. Before he could decide between signing off with 'yours faithfully' and 'sincerely yours', the bus had arrived at the stop that was right next to Javed's apartment complex.

Javed lived in a sprawling three-bedroom duplex flat in the midget apartments of the city's municipal authority.

The apartment complex comprised some twenty-odd buildings arranged next to each other in rows. The flats were numbered to the thousandth place in a sequence that was designed to baffle anyone who hadn't grown up in that complex. (To locate the complex in the colony itself, one needed to remember to add to the aforementioned four-digit number, a character and a letter, each denoting the sector and the pocket.) Alice had come here about ten times before but had trouble locating apartment 5163, first floor.

He asked the watchman, a newbie, for directions—prompting the watchman to bare his yellowing, crooked teeth, giggle and act coy for a while. Then, realizing he would get no tip, he threw his hand about, here and there, vaguely mumbling some explanations, confusing Alice more than he already was. Alice walked ahead and asked a few more people who shooed him away irritably. He finally located the flat behind an angry resident who insisted the number was part of a different sector altogether. When Alice showed him the number behind his head, he grew angrier. 'Then why did you ask me, motherfucker?' he snarled at Alice and walked away in a huff.

Flat number 5163 was a handsome-looking flat with creepers tastefully arching a beautiful wooden door. The flat belonged to Javed's parents, who were insanely rich and lived roughly two thousand kilometres away. They were rich enough for Javed to live as an amateur photographer—PhD ongoing for seven years—the kind who took up projects only when fancy seized him. Most of the time, though, he procrastinated, lazed around, and wrote a somewhat popular blog decrying the decay of the city's art scene. His constant lament was that exhibitions were no longer about art but about wine, starters and socializing. Alice maintained that art had always been about just that. 'Renaissance was just one long Lodhi Road through Europe.' The flat was in one of the more expensive colonies and so would have fetched nearly a lakh per month in rent. The fact that someone would forego that much just to house one's jobless son, encouraging him, in effect, to lead a life of further joblessness, never ceased to amaze Alice.

The door opened before Alice even rang the bell. Javed, clad in a simple kurta-pyjama despite the weather, grinned and said, 'I saw you from the balcony, but I thought I'll call out to you only if you start to go out in search of the next sector.' The house was neat thanks to a full-time manservant, a middle-aged man named Chhotu, presently out on an errand.

Once Chhotu returned, they lunched at the dining table, catching up on the affairs of each other's lives—they hadn't met in a few weeks—while being served hot kebabs and rotis.

'Abbi has been bugging me again about marriage. I have managed to ward off the disaster for the time being, but I have a feeling it might resurface very soon.'

'Why don't you want to get married? Aren't you close to thirty now?'

Javed pondered the question for a while.

'I don't feel thirty. I am Jack's wasted youth.' He immediately burst out laughing. Then he said, 'Besides, don't you know I've always wanted to live as an ascetic?'

Alice made a show of taking a good hard look at all the expensive items—the cutlery and the range of dishes made for lunch included—in the house, and then the house itself. Javed laughed soundlessly throughout and then said, 'Listen, all the great ascetics led princely lives before giving it all up. They also marry some poor sucker only to abandon her and the litter. I am breaking the cycle.'

'Is this ascetic life connected to your plan of starting a religion?' asked Alice. Javed, when spent, was in the habit of making elaborate plans of starting a religion that would bring about a great revolution in the country and consequently the world.

'Yes, yes, it is. It's all coming together. There are still parts I need to figure out. Let me explain—' Javed took on a professorial air.

'Please don't,' Alice countered hurriedly. 'I need to be really stoned to be able to listen to you talk about your religion.'

'Trust me,' said Javed, 'it's really interesting.'

'Javed, we have very different ideas of what is interesting,' insisted Alice. 'Why don't we finish lunch, roll a joint and then you can get down to explaining it to me.'

'Fine. But when you are already excitable on pot, my ideas might just push you over the edge and not just blow your mind, but destroy it,' drawled Javed.

'Looking forward to it,' mumbled Alice and turned his attention to the delicious navratan korma, which was Chhotu's specialty.

~

'Don't you think Ajatashatru is a really cool name? I think Ajatashatru is a really cool name,' cooed Alice. Being spent was contentment.

Javed continued to flip the pages of a really fat book. His bedroom was dark, slightly untidy, and smelt of Classic Milds and marijuana. The wall opposite the door was filled, edge to edge, with numerous photographs of all shapes, sizes and hues, its subjects spilling out from one frame into the other, creating a series of badly defined segments exploding into one large canvas of artwork. Even though he lived there alone and had given Alice no reason to think that he was anything other than asexual, his room sported a classy double bed, with antique bedside tables with an antique lamp atop each on either side. Other walls were sporadically covered with posters that he had commissioned Alice to design for him whenever Alice had run out of money, which was very often.

'Ajatashatru! You should change your name to Ajatashatru. See how nice even saying it feels,' smiled Alice, his eyes nearly closing.

'If it feels nice to say it, why would I name myself that?' asked Javed. 'I hardly ever use my own name.'

Alice found it very difficult to understand what Javed had said, so he ignored the bits he couldn't comprehend and said, 'You should use your name more often. It's a nice name ... Ajatashatru ... not Javed ... Javed is a shitty name... Don't Muslims usually have nicer names ... Tassawwur ... or Mustafa...? They are also better looking than you... Have you noticed, Javed? Does it give you a complex? Being a plain-looking Muslim? Is it stressful? Is that why you are trying to define yourself through ascetic pursuits?'

Javed finally found the page he was looking for. 'See this is from the *Digha Nikaya*, one of Buddhism's ancient sacred texts. There are two competing ways of looking at how things, or life—even existence itself—unfolds. There is the popular Karma theory of cause and effect, of course, but the Buddhists had another way of seeing these things: Pratityasamutpada or the theory of codependent origination.'

'O! Ajatashatru! Please explain in simple terms,' sang Alice, stretching his arms out with great effort. 'I am of small mind and smaller penis. Please don't perturb me with such details.'

Javed sniggered despite his annoyance and then took a deep breath, moving his hands about to dramatically centre himself.

'Okay, focus,' he told himself and then turned to Alice. 'You know how you upper-caste Hindu boys, on reaching teen age and learning of the horrors of the caste system decide to have a brief dalliance through your youth with Buddhism?'

'What brief dalliance?' cried Alice, indignantly. 'I still pray to Buddha Avalokiteswara. And Parsvanath.'

'I thought you go there for the Jain pizzas. You are the only weirdo I know who voluntarily craves Jain pizzas.'

'The rich taste of Ahimsa. Mmmm...' Alice smiled and swayed slowly.

'Also why do you pray? Didn't you tell me you were an atheist or something?' Javed was still turning pages, perhaps in an attempt to find something that would be simple enough to just read out.

Alice had forgotten that he had told Javed he was an atheist. He had told both his mother and later, Bakchod, that he prayed to Buddhist and Jain gods because he wasn't too sure they would want to live with a complete apostate. But he didn't want to go to the really crowded temples every Tuesday and Thursday either. 'Well, not pray, you know,' Alice tried to explain. 'What's the atheist version of praying? It's like ... you know ... it's like saying, Dear Bodhisattva or Parsva, *I know* that you don't exist-slash-died thousands of years ago and can't really hear me, but ... you know I just want you to know that I dig your philosophy and it's really cool, that, you know, thousands ... I mean that, fucking thousands of years ago, you just totally like opposed superstitions and promoted scientific temper and other constitutional values even though it was so, you know, far back in the day. We didn't even have a Constitution. But still you did it. So, I just want to say: Whoa! Whatte guy! You know, that kind of prayer.'

'Okay, please stop talking shit. I will just try and explain what I mean in very very simple words if you will just stop talking.'

'Yeah, you need to start talking. Otherwise, I'll just keep…'

Javed closed the book and put it away. He sat up straight and assumed a very professorial look.

'The theory of Karma is so popular, not just in India, but around the world, because it's such a simple and easy-to-digest idea: cause and effect. But it's also so potent because it doesn't just stop at that. It's cause and effect across lifetimes, on an eternal scale. And in ancient India, during what is called the second wave of urbanization in the subcontinent, there were an umpteen number of ascetic traditions: ninety-six, the Pali texts say. All of them had their own take on Karma. Some rejected it altogether while others broadly agreed to it and went on to develop their own unique version of it.

'People who believed in the theory of Karma were obsessed with figuring out a way of life that one could live without leaving a residue of karma. The perfect balancing of accounts. A way of life where the good and bad cancel each other out so perfectly that you achieve singularity.

No more birth or death. Some ascetics or Sramanas who didn't believe in Karma developed various other ideas. Ajivikas, for instance, believed, not in karma but in a kind of determinism. They believed that the web of factors that dictate how things unfold is beyond human control. And so, everything that happens is preordained and unchangeable.'

Alice surprised himself by being able to follow all this. 'So there's one tradition that holds us accountable for things that we probably have no control over, while the other exempts us from responsibility for everything.'

Javed nodded. 'Succinctly put. All of this is philosophy, right? There are two extremes: taking responsibility for everything, and taking responsibility for nothing.'

Alice furrowed his brows. 'So your religion purports to find the middle ground between the two? And thereby be the perfect synthesis of these two ideas?'

Javed scowled. 'What? No! That's more philosophy. Religion is not about finding synthesis. Religion is about gatekeeping. My religion will gatekeep the kind of causes people have to take responsibility for and the causes people can just shrug off. The total commitment to truth is the fault of philosophy. Religion has that leeway which is utterly necessary to making a huge group of people follow something.'

Alice was impressed. 'Okay, I am not totally regretting listening to you. So you're going to invent a religion that is branded as a combination of Buddhism and Jainism...'

Javed put his hand up to stop Alice and shook his head vigorously. 'See, even Buddhism and Jainism had and continue to have political forms that are just as unsavoury as any other political religion. The best of what we admire in Buddhism is actually linked to the Sramana tradition. This is the tradition that opposed both the caste system and the karmic justification for caste. And the Sramana ascetic tradition is not restricted to just Buddhism and Jainism. Most of the ninety six religions which were a part of the Mahajanapada age merged into what is now called Hinduism.'

Alice closed his eyes and tried to follow the thread of logic with some effort. 'So you are talking about reviving an extinct religion that doesn't have the baggage of Buddhism, Jainism and Hinduism...'

Javed nodded. 'Or Islam or Christianity or Zoroastrianism. A religion lost so long ago in history that it can claim to have never been corrupted. But whatever we know must also be tantalizing enough to generate widespread or even cult-like interest.'

'Hmmm, so something that's rooted in the Indian tradition but is also not besmirched by caste.' Alice had to admit that Javed was on to something. Javed only used to spout long rants about his own ideas of faith and progress, which although not suspect or ill thought out, carried no ideological heft on account of being the ideas of an unknown nobody. If he could back them up even with suggestions of historicity, he could go very far with the kind of money he had to back himself up. 'What is this mysterious, lost religion that you are talking about? To be absolutely, one hundred per cent honest, if you show me an intriguing, extinct religion, I will adopt it like it's a kitten getting wet in the rain.'

Javed looked pleased. 'Okay. There were several religions that belonged to the Sramana tradition. Buddhism and Jainism are the only two that survive to the present day. Ajivikism, or the Ajivika religion, is no longer practised and is therefore perfect to reimagine as we see it. Some writers believe this is actually an ancient religion that predates Buddhism and may have influenced the Buddha to adopt radically egalitarian politics. The Ajivika religion was never a major political force even in the Mahajanapada age, and its followers suffered persecution in the first millennium AD leading to its extinction by the Middle Ages. But what's really interesting is that some academics who have studied the religion in terms of its philosophy stretch its origins back to the Indus Valley Civilization.' He patted the monstrous book that sat in his lap.

Alice sat up excitedly. 'Are you fucking serious? That sounds really kickass. I am sorry for mocking thee, O Ajatashatru. This is indeed worth reading big books for. Where can I find more information?'

'This book is a treasure trove. For instance, the set-up to explaining the Ajivika religion is so well done because the time period in which the religion becomes popular is given a lot of importance. The period itself was an interesting time in the history of world religions. While the Bronze Age civilizations in the third and second millennia BCE saw a tribe-based city-state pantheon of gods and goddesses, the first millennium saw the rise of world religions. Zoroastrianism, Judaism, Christianity, Buddhism, Jainism, Ajivikism, Confucianism, Taoism and so on. Basically, religions that sought to unite working classes across ethnicity in urban areas. The basis of their confluence was shared material experiences. They became world religions because these shared material experiences were universal. It was a huge shift from the way religion was imagined before that. In that context, the word Ajivika is especially significant because Ajivika means "wage-earner". This religion's name betrays the target audience.'

Javed, satisfied that his little monologue would have piqued Alice's interest sufficiently, picked up a thinner book from the shelf. 'You could start with this. Then, there are eight volumes of comparative religious philosophy to get through.'

Alice sighed. 'You know what. I think the name is enough for now. I'll Google the rest.'

Javed laughed. 'You'll find nothing on Google.'

'I'll make do with what I find. I don't need to know much. I trust you. You work on the revolution, I will do the posters. Okay?'

'Fair enough. Just make nice posters. I am tired of you retro-fitting Cold War communist propaganda posters for the socially important causes of today.' He pointed in the general direction of the posters he meant to refer to.

Alice sighed dramatically. 'Yeah. You know, once you start figuring out politics, you start to realize that a lot of things you thought were okay are actually really offensive and politically incorrect. And the more you learn about politics the more you realize that things we think are okay are really not OKAY.' Alice had worked himself up with that rant. He sat up with purpose. 'This is not OKAY, Javed. You need to start a revolution and fix these things. Fuck the system up, you know. Bring on the Ajivika revolution. I am starting to get really invested in this. How soon are you starting the revolution? Will the message fit in 180 characters?'

Javed scratched his ear and yawned. 'I really should be working on my thesis, but since I am never going to do that, I am working on reconstructing Ajivika mythology, cosmology and philosophy from existing sources.'

'Like, all existing sources.'

Javed waved his hand around at the bookshelves on either side of the bed. 'There are only about five complete scholarly works on the Ajivikas due to a paucity of original sources. Some scholars have attempted reconstructions by comparative religious methods, but even those books aren't more than twenty. I bought them all.'

'All of them?' Alice asked.

'Every one of them. At least every book that I know of. If I find there are more books, I'll get those too. Getting rare books has become so easy thanks to eBay.' Javed smiled with contentment.

'No. Getting rare books is easy for you thanks to money. That website is just there to get you rich buggers to spend the damn money.'

'Wah, comrade,' said Javed, grinning. 'Maybe *you* will be the rock upon which I build my church.'

'What church?' asked Alice, thoroughly confused. 'I thought the Ajivikas were ascetics.'

'No, what I mean is,' Javed tried to explain patiently, 'you will be my foremost apostle. The carrier of my gospel.'

'If I am the apostle, then who is The Rock?' Alice scratched his head to irritate Javed. 'These mixed religious metaphors are too much for my spent state. Can we stick to one religion?'

Javed took a deep breath, as if to calm himself, and sighed. 'Forget about all that. Are you sold on the religion? Can I count you as my first convert?'

Alice stuck an open palm to his right temple in salute. 'Ji, huzoor. From today, I am Rock, the apostle. Carrier of gospels and crusher of marijuana. Can we smoke another one? I don't think I can sleep with all this excitement. I need to pass out.'

As Alice crushed some more pot, Javed began to make preparations to roll the joint and the conversation jumped from topic to topic as it often does when two people talk at each other after getting spent. While filling the joint with a crushed blend of marijuana and tulsi, Javed appeared to become a little more pensive. After he had finished up rolling the joint, he asked, 'Did you do anything about getting her number? What's that kid's name?'

Javed knew Snigdha's name, but it was part of the show he put up to make sure Alice didn't interpret Javed's curiosity as caring. Alice did get Snigdha's number from Iyengar but had no idea about how to begin the conversation. His friends had suggested a variety of ways. But no matter how he imagined the text to go, all of those scenarios somehow ended with Snigdha calling him a creep and asking him to fuck off.

'I have her number, but I don't want to text her, okay? I can't. I physically can't.'

'What's the worst that—'

'Don't say that. I really don't understand why people say that. How is "what's the worst that could happen" any kind of a motivator? How do you propose to get someone to do something by getting him to imagine the worst possible consequence? Who comes up with this shit?'

'Okay. Think about the best thing that could happen.'

'I really haven't been trained to think in terms of best-case scenarios. Let me think about this. She could say yes and also turn out to be a ridiculously rich person who just wants someone to love her for her, you know. And not the money. But, you know, she also has enough money. Enough that we can watch a movie in PVR *and* eat popcorn. Every week. And all of the days during the Oscar week.'

'Wow, you really dream big,' mocked Javed, clapping softly. 'All the same, that's not the worst thing to imagine. Think about it. If that's the best possible scenario, don't you feel like you must try to talk to her, no matter what?'

Alice sat up. 'My god! You are right, Javed. I need to message her. Or meet her again. Or something. She's Iyengar's friend. I should organize a party or something and get Iyengar to invite her again. I should do something.'

'Bah, finally,' exclaimed Javed. 'What's wrong with you? Why did I have to push you into this?'

'Because it's easier to get spent and fantasize about a perfect relationship than to actually pursue one, okay? What do you think *you* do all the time? Do you make an effort, or do you just mope around reading books and not getting laid? You are literally starting a religion, so you don't have to be in a relationship.'

'The difference is that you actually met someone, you dimwit. Anyway, now that I've converted you to the Ajivika faith, my job here is done. Actually, I am sleeping in this room, so *your* job here is done. Chhotu would have put the blankets out in the guest bedroom for you. Scoot.'

Alice danced out of the room ecstatic that he had found a cool new religion he could claim to be a part of. It was an ancient Indian tradition, so even though it wasn't Hindu it would still pass the scrutiny of both his mother and Bakchod.

As he lay in bed waiting for sleep, he marvelled at the marketability of Javed's Ajivikism. It was old and obscure enough that it couldn't be properly tied to casteism. Unlike Buddhism, which, even though considered progressive in India or the West, gets bad press from Sri Lanka or Myanmar, Ajivikism wasn't even an extant religion. All the best liberal fantasies could be retro projected on to it to one's heart's content. He could almost hear one of his uncles say something like: Do you know both men and women could take Ajivika vows? It was a feminist religion. Do you know Ajivika means wage-earner? It was clearly a working-class religion. Communism didn't start with that Marx fellow, it started in ancient India.

Javed had an extremely viable cult on his hands and Alice, as the foremost apostle, would be the rock upon which Javed would build his church. Alice was thoroughly excited by the idea of working as a zealot like those missionaries back home who made the lives of pedestrians miserable every Sunday morning. Anything to avoid a nine-to-five job. And being able to piss people off was just a cherry on the icing.

3

'Krav Maga is basically a counterattack and self-defence system developed by the Israelis. It is supposed to be really potent, you know. And I expect it *would* be since somebody or the other is always fucking with the Jews. First the Egyptians, then Hitler and now the Arabs. How do I know it's great? I saw a Krav Maga video on YouTube, man. It's so awesome it's not even funny. I bet that anybody who learnt it could kick the shit out of whomever they wanted. They apparently teach it at Siri Fort, in the mornings. What do you say?' Bakchod loved to sell stuff.

Alice, staunch in his support for Palestine, expressed his disinterest with a soft cluck. 'I don't know, man. Martial arts is not for people like me. Firstly, it'll involve making a time commitment, which I am not okay with. Secondly, I don't think I would ever want to beat anybody up.'

'What if, hypothetically, the guy you could beat up was this smug bastard on a Pulsar wearing a tight T-shirt?'

'Hmm. Hypothetically, does his Pulsar have radium stickers and LED bling?'

'Not just that, he also has a sticker that reads "Jat on Hunt" or something like that, on the license plate.'

'Oh yeah! I'd definitely want to beat him up.'

Alice had just returned from work and was making idle conversation with Bakchod who was waiting for his girlfriend to log on to Skype. Bakchod tried to appear nonchalant and engage in general jabber, but sitting a few feet away from his laptop, his eyes would dart every now and then towards his laptop screen with a look of hope that would be momentarily extinguished. With each subsequent glance, the faint frown on his handsome face grew more prominent. Alice laughed in his head as he sat near the door, smoking a cigarette, and shivered on and off: Bakchod had a rule that disallowed smoking with the door closed and wisps of ice-cold air made their way into the room, and pierced his face and hands. His brain told him that his nostrils probably looked like entrances to caves since the snot in his nose would certainly have crystallized and arranged itself into icicles. Providing the background score to their conversation was a particularly angst-ridden A.R. Rahman, who, with complete disregard for the population density of the country, was passionately exhorting expats to return home in *'Yeh jo des hai tera'*.

'Okay, how about this? The guy has gelled hair and drives an SUV,' said Bakchod. 'Would you want to beat him up?'

'Does he sport a stubble and wear aviators?'

'No, but his second language in school was French.'

'Oh yeah! I'd want to beat the crap out of that guy. Eighteen whacks. One for each language in the Indian constitution he could have chosen instead of French.' He had been feeling vaguely patriotic ever since Bakchod started playing Bhagat Singh songs in the morning.

'Ha ha! Awesome!' laughed Bakchod. 'You should put this in your diary.'

The diary, a gift from Alice's father, was meant for the purpose of listing down his daily expenditures. Needless to say, his black diary never fulfilled its intended purpose. Instead, he tried to turn the diary into a collection of his weightiest musings. A black book, like Jung's red book, even. If, fingers crossed, he managed to contract some kind of psychosis, the diary could become a collectible. To this end, he made entries under differing states of intoxication; the kind that seemed brilliant at that moment but made him squirm with embarrassment upon attaining sobriety. Therefore, it became a personal journal of sorts where, under various headings, he listed out his likes and dislikes, for instance, his favourite movie quotes and exotic swear words in various languages since, according to him, humour, in general, was more agreeable than contemplative earnestness.

He skimmed through the pages looking for the correct title and stopped at 'Kinds of people I must hate'. This section had the most number of entries and ran for over four pages. On the fifth page were three entries:

People who say 'anyways' instead of 'anyway'.

People who use DSLRs.

People who like Guy Ritchie's *Sherlock Holmes*.

Under the last entry he quickly scribbled: 'People whose second language in school is/was French/ People whose school's name has the word "International" in it.' Bakchod chuckled his assent at the corollary. Now that the diary had been pulled out, they decided to go ahead and think of some more reasons to list inside it. Alice, being a stickler for quality control, decided that they must brainstorm before making any definitive entries, an endeavour that consumed the better part of the next half hour.

While Alice was goofing off with Bakchod, those who had attained adulthood were undoubtedly taking on freelance assignments and promptly dispatching deliverables to their clients. But Alice's proclivity for laziness and general inaction shielded him from similarly sound decisions that could have been made with regard to his career. He often blamed his parents for his lack of ambition: he had never had an opportunity to be exposed to any kind of financial hardship and therefore took a general degree of economic stability for granted. As far as greater degrees of material pleasures went, he was hard-pressed to imagine what might be a greater pleasure than sitting on the terrace and smoking a cigarette while talking shit with his friends or drinking beer clandestinely at the tea shack outside his college while bitching about his work to his college mates. Everyone else maintained that greater pleasures existed, and perhaps they really did, so he blamed cable TV for his inability to imagine what they might be. He had managed to put down, thus, his lack of ambition to ineffective fostering by his mother, father and television.

During his more contemplative moods, dissatisfied with the simplicity of the aforementioned reasons and in response to his father's question: 'Don't you feel lost, just drifting along with no sense of purpose?', he came up with a reason that helped to reinforce his arguments. The idea cascaded into his brain while reading *An Idiot's Guide to Søren Kierkegaard*. He had once explained it (to Bakchod) thus: 'Look at it this way, man. You'll become a big businessman, earn a lot of money, live a splendid life. I'll laze around, not give a fuck and live a fairly mediocre life. You'll be happy in your own way, and I'll probably be fucked. Then, some fifty years later, we'll both die. A hundred and fifty years after that, anyone who has ever known us, directly or indirectly, will die. And even if you brought global peace and finished the 14th level of Claw without cheat codes and isolated the Higgs boson, all in one day, you'll be forgotten in a thousand years, give or take. A few hundred thousand more years from that, mankind itself will have ceased to exist. A few billion years from that, the earth itself will perish and a trillion years later, the entire universe. So, do you see how pointless your "purposeful" ambitions are from an ontological standpoint?'

Thoroughly enthused by his own eloquence in this line of thought, he had quickly pulled out his black diary and reasoned his lack of career ambitions in black and triumphantly titled it 'Existential Apathy: A Reason to Eliminate All Reason'.

Presently, Bakchod's laptop emitted a fake landline ring indicating that Neha had logged in.

'Hi baby, do you know how long you made me wait?'

'Sorry, babes. Class got over late today.'

Alice took this as a cue to leave. He had run out of cigarettes in any case, and so decided to go out to fetch some more. He put on his muffler—a gift from his ex-girlfriend, Ananya. Timely, too, since it had been given to him the previous winter. While Bakchod and Neha discussed the inanities of each other's lives, Alice stood in front of the mirror trying to gauge the displacement from the centre of the scalp that would be optimum for parting his thick, wavy and currently unmanageable hair. Realizing that there was nothing much he could do about his hair short of shaving it off, he picked his bag up and walked out into the cold.

It was a busy night and the taillights of mist-obscured vehicles gave the roads a psychedelic air. The road that bent thrice to take Alice from his building to the college radiated frigidity like an overzealous air conditioner. Cars with misty windows zoomed up and down the road, on the sides of which, watchmen, sitting around the small fires they had made, chatted while petting stray dogs that lay at their feet. A few motorcyclists, armed with sweaters and windcheaters, braved the cold but drove at low speeds, while pedestrians walked briskly with hands buried deep into their pockets. From the college gate, the road made a beeline for the State Bank of India ATM and thereupon split three ways before diffusing further. The tea shack opposite the college gate was the place, where students and ex-students gathered for a smoke. It was therefore christened—rather unimaginatively—Suttah Point. A makeshift shop of sorts, it sold cigarettes, biscuits, chips, Maggi and bread-omelette. There was also a ubiquitous supply of tea, of course. Next to the shop were a few slabs of stone propped up by a couple of bricks for the customers to sit on; the compound wall of the park beyond served as a back-rest for them.

As Alice walked closer to college, the bright streetlights revealed Ravi, Kaamya and Biswas chatting animatedly with Nitin who, upon noticing Alice, waved at him with a broad smile and beckoned him to hurry up and join the conversation. Alice greeted the shop owner, Sanju, the tea maker, and occupied an empty slab after wiping off the dew on it with his bag. Kaamya and Ravi, who were sitting arm in arm, smiled at him and proceeded to prop themselves up even closer to each other and snuggle, making him wonder if they expected him to rate their love for each other like a judge on a reality show!

Biswas smiled, raised a hand and said, in Bengali, 'Your penis looks very beautiful.' Alice grinned and replied, also in Bengali, 'Your penis looks very beautiful, too.' This unusual form of greeting between two verifiably heterosexual friends traced its origin back to a rather boring class (Application of Intellectual Property Rights to something or the other) in the second year of college. That day, their shrill teacher had just discovered that the majority of the class had re submitted their seniors' case-studies and had built herself up into a rage. Being chronic backbenchers, Alice and Biswas were seated in the last row of their classroom, sharing a desk. As her light eyes shone with demented anger and her mouth emitted shrieks that beckoned apocalypse, they engaged in a tense game of six-men-a-side book cricket. They had made a deal that if Sachin Gangu-vaskar, who was on Alice's team, scored fifty runs in consecutive sixes, Biswas would have to teach him one sentence of Bengali each day for a whole year. Being fond of learning new languages, Alice opened the pages of 'Letters to Penthouse XIV' with a rare dexterity that allowed his number eleven, Gangu-vaskar, to score a record-breaking 378 runs with fifties scored in consecutive sixes about three times. With the teacher still shrieking, Biswas opened the last page of his notebook and scrawled a note in a corner: 'I will teach you how to compliment another person's penis in Bengali.' Alice, suppressing a laugh, had scribbled back, 'Sounds like something I'll want to say to lot of Bengali people. Go ahead.'

After the teacher had finally shut up, Alice and Bakchod, en route to the canteen, went into the loo to piss. The toilet had three urinals, and the one in the middle had been occupied by a lanky Sardar in a red turban and a full-armed shirt. Alice and Biswas occupied the urinals on either side of him. Believing that this was the best time to use his newly learnt phrase, Alice smiled at Biswas with mock coyness and said, 'Tumhar bara khoob shundor laagchchi.' Biswas had probably been about to return the compliment, when the Sardar suddenly zipped up and turning to Alice, and whispered in a chillingly soft voice, 'What the fuck is going on? You think you can say whatever the hell you like since you think I do not understand Bangla?' and proceeded to rattle out a few sentences in Bengali, all of which escaped Alice's comprehension. This most unfortunate example of Murphy's Law surprised Alice and the fear of the Bong-Surd made him stop mid-stream. Zipping up, he stammered several apologies in English and insisted that he was unaware of the meaning of what he had just said. The Bong-Surd refused to listen to any of this and continued to blast Alice in Bengali. Biswas looked thunderstruck, but he recovered in time to tell the Bong-Surd, in chaste Bengali, that Alice was a repressed homo from a very conservative family and was just adjusting to his new-found freedom in the college. The Bong-Surd looked highly unconvinced, but perhaps let them go thinking that so outlandish an explanation probably had to be true. Since then, in memory of that terrifying, unique and therefore hilarious (in retrospect) incident, Alice and Biswas would greet each other by complimenting each other's penises. Alice did not learn a word of Bengali beyond that, but this one sentence, he never forgot.

Presently, Biswas turned to Sanju, and called for two double chais and a cigarette. The radio in the shack was playing one of Alice's favourite film songs: *'ILU ka matlab I love you, I love you, I love you…'*

Sanjay pulled out a saucepan where a lump of moist tea dust sat contentedly in a corner. He dug out two more spoons of tea dust from a PET bottle and threw it into the saucepan. Adding a few cups of water and a measured cup of milk to the sludge, he set it on the stove, stirring it from time to time. Alice had never seen the saucepan empty; there was always a pre-used lump of tea dust in it. It was perhaps Sanjay's way of reminding his customers of the transferrable nature of one's actions: cause and effect. That one's present was always a consequence of the past, that the past could not be wished away no matter what. Alice looked at Sanjay stirring the tea while scratching his pate and thought he did seem the deeply philosophical type.

'I was just about to message you,' said Nitin after a while, breaking Alice's reverie. 'Padma will be here in a while and she is bringing Snigdha along. She apparently told Snigdha about Suttah Point, and kind of FOMO-ed her into wanting to have Maggi and bread-omelette here.'

'Wow! This is great news,' said Alice with a wide smile, barely able to contain his joy. It had been about a week and a half since the night of the bonfire and the near incarceration. Alice had been trying to convince his brain to file Snigdha away as a passing crush of no great relevance. But there was a lot about her that had made a strong impression on him, and he found himself thinking about her quite often. And then the conversation with Javed inspired him to action when he was spent, but on attaining sobriety, he decided to do nothing about it.

'By the way, does Iyengar know that I have a crush on her?'

'No. Even I had no idea you had a crush on Iyengar.'

Alice ignored him and continued, 'Why am I even asking? Of course, she did. What did she say?' Nitin gave him a benign smile. 'Padma says she noticed it during the bonfire itself. You tend to speak in a different accent and stress certain syllables unnecessarily when you're trying to impress a girl. Her observation, not mine,' he added hurriedly in response to Alice's raised eyebrow. 'She asked me to tell you that she approves of you hitting on Snigdha, whatever that means. And I gather from her latest message that Snigdha asked if you were going to be there too. I have no idea in what context, but you can read too much into it if you like.'

'Don't mind if I do.' Alice grinned as a pleasant warmth spread through his entire body. He was glad he was dark because if his complexion were about three shades lighter, Nitin would have noticed that he was blushing. 'I had an awful day at work and I really need this. Damn! I should've worn my leather jacket. This is definitely not one of my better sweaters. It's frayed. Dark blue doesn't suit me, does it? What do you think? I sound like a teenage girl, don't I?'

Although he was past twenty-two and was a couple of relationships old, his response to early stages of courtship was shamefully adolescent in nature. He pulled his sleeves over his palms, flattened his hair over his ears and asked, 'Do I at least look somewhat like Kurt Cobain?'

As they sat there drinking tea, a few more of their friends started to trickle in with tired eyes and red noses. Nitin and Biswas chatted with them; mostly pleasant conversation sprinkled generously with passionate vulgarity when the topic demanded it. Alice, oblivious to the socializing around him, sat there fervently strategizing the evening. He would speak to her casually, he decided, with just the right amount of wit. Nothing too over the top; just a few casual jokes thrown in here and there. But what if he was too casual and seemed uninterested? Would that be a good thing? What percentage of measured disinterest amounted to cool nonchalance as opposed to withdrawn self-involvement?

As Alice sat there wrestling socio-romantic subtleties, an autorickshaw screeched to a halt in front of them with Iyengar and Snigdha in it. He stood up as the girls climbed on to the platform, immediately felt stupid about getting up since no one else had, pretended to dust the underside of his pants and sat down again just as Snigdha stretched her hand out. He ended up shaking it awkwardly from a half-seated position. Iyengar sat next to Nitin, and Snigdha sat on a flat stone in front of them. Iyengar made the introductions. 'Guys, this is Snigdha. She is my colleague and one of the very few girls I know who can hold her whisky. And, Snigdha, these are Ravi, Kaamya and Biswas. Ravi and Kaamya are entrepreneurs. I know, really disgusting. Biswas is a lifestyle journalist who is trying to bang out a novel before his older brother can complete his PhD, so he will not be referred to as the black sheep of his family behind his back, or, more importantly, to his face.'

'What's the book about?' asked Snigdha.

'Ummm … uhhhh…' Biswas hesitated. His manner seemed like that of someone who had been asked to bend over. Finally, he said, 'It's slice of life, you know. About a Bengali guy, trying to make it as a writer in Delhi.'

'Bengalis writing about Delhi can be a genre in itself, no?' grinned Snigdha.

Biswas laughed very loudly, making Alice want to throttle him. But Snigdha, to his relief, turned away from Biswas and asked him, 'Who are the others? Are they your college-mates too?'

She was wearing a beige jacket and a black turtleneck sweater over tapered jeans and had her hair tied in a ponytail. A pair of spectacles sat on her nose, giving her an air of seriousness that made her more attractive in Alice's eyes. The other day, at the time of the bonfire, she had probably worn contact lenses.

'Very few outsiders come here. All of us are from college,' explained Alice. 'Since graduation, about fifteen of us have been coming here regularly, perhaps trying to clutch at a kind of life that is now beyond our reach. We were part of different departments and barely knew each other, but in the last three months we have become an unlikely gang, a kind of support group for victims of college withdrawal. We become more social with each other once a little hooch has flown as you will see shortly.'

Snigdha seemed excited by the prospect of alcohol. Iyengar cleared her throat to indicate the introductions were incomplete.

'That is Abhiram,' continued Iyengar, pointing at a tall, long-haired guy with a goatee. 'He is a photographer and is generally very silent. Trying to engage him in conversation is Vikram. He is probably trying to convince Abhiram to do a profile shoot of one of his many lady-friends. Vinod and Item are Vikram's roommates. They must be on their way back from work and are probably buying beer and rum. Where is Rohit? Oh yeah, there he is chatting with that girl. She isn't the one Vikram came here with yesterday, is she? Hard to tell. They all look the same.'

All the girls that Vikram dated looked like they were made in an assembly line and poured out like effluents from the wealthier parts of the city.

By around quarter to eight, Bakchod turned up and so had most of the regulars. Vinod and Item had arrived about fifteen minutes earlier, bringing along with them a bottle of Old Monk rum and two six packs of Tennet's XXX Super Strong beer. Vikram and Item spiked a couple of bottles of Pepsi with the rum and passed them around. Alice, Bakchod and a few others opened the beer cans, hid them behind their bags and took long swigs while keeping a weather eye out for policemen. Snigdha picked up a spiked bottle of Pepsi, took a long sip, scowled as the drink went down her throat and said, 'You people drink a lot, don't you?'

Bakchod laughed and replied, 'Over the last couple of months I have often marvelled at not the quantity of alcohol I consume—which rarely goes beyond a can or two of beer most of the times—but how frequently I consume it. We drink here on almost all weekdays, and on Saturday nights there is the bonfire and booze on the terrace. Sunday nights, we usually end up finishing off the booze left over from Saturday, if any, before sleeping.'

Kaamya nodded and added, 'Most of us who are here outside college every evening, hang out with each other only because we find ourselves in the same physical space. I don't even like a lot of the people I hang out with but just do it out of a kind of lethargy. Like, I hate Vikram with a passion.'

'Why?' asked Snigdha.

'He's a pig. Stay away from him,' said Kaamya without offering further explanation. Alice felt a rush of gratitude towards Kaamya.

As conversation progressed, the traffic on the road gradually reduced and a thin curtain of smog descended upon the terrain rendering separate the thick bands of orange streetlights and the chalk bands of moonlight that fought their way through the trees.

The primary agenda for conversation amongst them was 'story-topping' that entailed people explaining in sufficient detail how much one's life sucked. The others would then, one by one, through concocted anecdotes and wild exaggerations, try to top the previous story and establish oneself as the most wretched of the lot. What had started off, a couple of months ago, as mewls of self-pity, quickly became a comparison of each one's endurance. When even endurance became commonplace, the stories became all about the masochistic pleasure each one took, when life decided to bugger them, in the said buggering. Vikram was usually disqualified from these discussions since his cousin's recent death and the disappearance of his pet dog amid the confusion of the grief that had ensued following the death, had provided him with an unfair advantage. The stories flowed with renewed vigour owing to the fact that there was a stranger in their midst, someone who was not familiar with the others' tales of woe.

The stories were funny and conversation enjoyable until Kaamya told them the tale of her boss grabbing her arse in the elevator. As a result, the conversation deviated from story-topping to sexual harassment and inevitably on to the patriarchal nature of society. Ravi, who had obviously heard the story before, mumbled dire threats directed at the boss, while Iyengar and Snigdha made several important remarks with a good deal of ardour. The others, almost all male, seized either by a vague and irrational sense of guilt, uncomfortable disinterest or both, became phrasal, then monosyllabic and ultimately refrained from speaking altogether. Snigdha, Iyengar and Kaamya spoke at length on the topic, discussed various plans of action and finally decided that Kaamya must report the matter first to higher-ups in the organization before taking it to the police. Alice was pissed off with Kaamya for breaking the unspoken code of Suttah Point talks: keep it funny, stupid and unimportant. Consequently, the mood became sombre and everybody was glad when the alcohol began to gnaw unpleasantly at their empty stomachs. Most of them made their way to a nearby dhaba for dinner. Alice, Bakchod, Nitin, Iyengar and Snigdha decided to stay back and ordered omelettes, bread and Maggi for themselves.

After the food arrived, they alternated between various topics including college nostalgia. The conversation then turned to Nitin's Bangalore plans.

'I have given it a lot of thought,' he said, picking at his Maggi contemplatively, 'and it seems the best move, career-wise.' He suddenly became emphatic. 'I can't believe I even thought about it for nearly a week! Anyone else in my place would have jumped at the offer.'

'Did you quit your job?'

'I filed my papers today. My one-month notice begins tomorrow.'

'Has Padma made her peace with it?' asked Snigdha with a smile.

'Oh yeah! It's always career before personal life for me, so it would be unfair to hold him to different rules,' said Iyengar. 'Besides, we seem to be turning into one of those clingy couples. Some distance might do us good.'

'Alice, meanwhile, is alternating between the five stages of grief,' quipped Bakchod, earning an elbow in the ribs for his effort. Massaging his ribs, he continued, 'So, Snigdha, when is your "getting gay with tigers" project starting?'

She laughed and began to detail her plans. She spoke seriously and with passion, clearly proud of what she was setting out to do. Even Bakchod, who held all animals, except for fish, in mild contempt, soon began to take an interest in what she had to say.

Alice's mind turned to things that were bothering him through the last couple of weeks. First, Nitin's decision to move to Bangalore, and now Snigdha's passion for her work—seemed to indicate that there was something people seemed to aspire after other than merely biding their time and waiting for things to happen to them. He felt he had been in perfect equilibrium—mildly happy with his books, music, his job and mildly unhappy with his stagnant social life, the nature of his work and the government in Andhra Pradesh—until Nitin and Snigdha upset this delicate balance, making him, much against his will, ask questions like, 'What do I want to do with my life?' and 'Where do I see myself three, five or ten years from now?' The typical job interview kind of questions that he would have pooh-poohed earlier began to make him wonder if they perhaps did have a significance towards which only he was impervious.

Everyone, it seemed to him, had an ambition. A clear and definite purpose with which to shape their lives and more importantly, take decisions of any kind. Nitin was invested enough in his work to leave behind a comfortable life, friends, girlfriend and set off to graze greener pastures. Snigdha was going to quit her high-paying job to follow her dreams of saving forests. Bakchod wanted to become insanely rich, means no bar. Suddenly, jokes about his apathy and a defining lack of interest in anything around him seemed insufficient. Was this an inevitable part of growing up, Alice wondered. His mood grew increasingly gloomy, and his demeanour, progressively withdrawn.

After stewing in vague gloom for a good half an hour, tired and frustrated by his own thoughts, he decided to tackle problems on the basis of immediacy. Since his so-called absence of purpose was certainly not immediate while impressing Snigdha was, he rejoined the conversation and spoke a lot. He did not manage to say a single funny or brilliant thing, but nothing he said was particularly stupid or squirm-worthy either. The overall effort was B–, his brain decided, which certainly exceeded expectations.

Time flew by as it usually does when nobody wants it to and soon it was time for Snigdha to leave. 'Should I wait for an auto right here?' she asked, slightly unsure. 'I haven't seen a vehicle pass this way in the last hour or so.' The alcohol had not dulled Alice's brain and he was quick to grab an opportunity when it presented itself. 'You'll have to wait at the bus stop,' he said. 'Come on, I'll walk you there.' He grabbed Nitin's jacket, which was lying in a heap by his side. Bakchod looked away with a pained expression on his face, which was, perhaps, the result of trying really hard not to laugh. Iyengar seemed to get up too, but a slight nudge from Nitin prompted her to say, 'I think the booze and food have made me really queasy.' She added a grimace, to make it more convincing. 'You don't mind if I don't tag along, do you?' Snigdha didn't seem to mind. 'No problem. Pop a mint, it'll help with the nausea. Thanks for an awesome dinner, people. Bye. Take care, Padma.'

~

Hands in pockets, they walked down the road towards the SBI ATM, with their heads slightly bowed to avoid the cold wind that was piercing their eyes. Alice was contemplating taking his muffler and wrapping it around his face as protection. Resisting the urge, he tried to start a conversation, but could only think of, 'Help! This damned wind is burrowing into my eyes and nostrils! Help!' Luckily, Snigdha spoke soon.

'You grew very silent and serious there for a while when I was talking about my project. Did I bore you terribly?'

'Ha ha, not at all. I was just dealing with some coming-of-age dilemmas. Nothing I can really do about them. Primarily, since they do not, yet, qualify as problems.'

'Still, you can tell me about them. Maybe I'll help nip them in the bud!'

'Okay, it's your funeral,' he said with a chuckle. 'See, when you started talking so passionately about your work, it just reminded me, unpleasantly, of the fact that I don't seem to be that interested in anything at all. Not just you; Nitin or Bakchod or Biswas—everybody seems to have something that steers them. Listening to you talk gave me this vague feeling that life was somehow just passing me by with no intervention on my part.'

They reached the ATM and turned right. A couple of streetlights on this road were dysfunctional, rendering it dark and dingy. The silence of the night was only broken by a nursing bitch that growled harmlessly from behind a pile of garbage bags. Their shadows travelled the breadth of the road and met a tree on the other side. They crossed it and continued walking.

'Surely this isn't the first time you have felt the need for an ambition of some sort. I am sure social pressures would have forced you to confront these questions much earlier. Why today then?'

'Who knows,' replied Alice. 'When the temperature falls, some animals tend to hibernate. I, on the other hand, tend to behave like a character in a Farhan Akhtar movie, I suppose. Only without any money.' All of a sudden, it came to Alice that he had wasted enough time talking about his vague idiotic problems when he should have been trying to be charming and funny instead; maybe even knowledgeable. No, that's a stretch, his brain pointed out. Okay, at least charming and funny.

Before he could say anything though, Snigdha, her head still bent to avoid the wind, said, 'What you want to do with your life or your sense of purpose, so to speak, does not come packaged in your DNA as a profession.' She took a deep breath and then continued, 'If you manage to stay aware of everything that you do, one of those things that you do will fire your frontal cortex more effectively than the others.'

Alice pondered this briefly. 'What you say does make sense. But believe me, everything that I do is, to me, an even grey. It starts off with a brilliant white, in the beginning, slowly begins to fade out and turns greyer and greyer as I get used to the work more and more. I get bored very easily. That's my problem.' Good, he managed to end it. More questions about her. No more talking, only smart, witty replies. 'Tell me about yourself, though, why tigers? Calvin and Hobbes fan?'

Snigdha laughed loudly and the laughter effervesced through the empty street. 'See, that's what I am saying: It is not the tigers. The indicator is less about profession and more about what one feels like in a certain environment.

For instance, the way I feel like when I am camping in the forest.'

'What exactly do you feel?' Alice asked, a little uncertain. She bent her head sideways and scratched the side of her neck contemplatively. Then she answered, 'Here, we are constantly trying to adjust our environment to suit us perfectly.' Alice unconsciously pulled both halves of Nitin's jacket closer and managed to thumb in a couple of buttons. She continued, 'Heaters in winters, coolers in summers. And needs go in degrees, right, so there is no such thing as absolute fulfilment. So, we keep tinkering with our surroundings step by step or by degrees, almost deliberately avoiding contentment. But in the wild there is a savagery that is sorely missing in our daily lives. To tame that savagery is impossible. And when you can't change what is outside, then the only thing you can change—'

'—is what is on the inside,' finished Alice, in a soft baritone.

Snigdha continued in the same tone, but there was a strange weight to her words now. 'It sounds very corny, but in essence, yes. You just sort of surrender to the savagery and make whatever changes you can to yourself. In this state you are at your most primal. Not modifying your surroundings to suit you but adapting to suit your surroundings. And I believe that's the only way to live, because, isn't that the way we evolved?'

How many girls did he know who thought like that, leave alone speak like that? Alice wanted to establish himself as an equal and not merely agree with Snigdha. He thought about it for a bit. 'You seem uncomfortable,' Snigdha said with a smile. 'Are you wondering if I am bullshitting you?'

'No, no. In fact, I agree with you in spirit. But here's the snag: evolution, savagery, et cetera, are great concepts, Snigdha, but what about our basic comforts? If happiness is to be our highest ideal, and I believe that it is, how can anyone be happy in discomfort?'

Her reply came immediately, as though she were expecting the question. 'Comfort is an issue only when survival can be taken for granted.' She had a slightly crooked smile on her face and there was a glint in her eye. In the darkness of the night, she looked almost dangerous. 'We try to behave like immortals. All of us. And when we do, we need distractions. But maybe just keep reminding yourself you could drop dead any second. Memento mori!'

They took another right turn and reached the bus stop. Midnight in the capital city was just the beginning of a new day. Alice spotted an empty auto almost immediately, at a distance, and waved his hand.

Fuck! he thought to himself. He would really need to up his game just to be able to talk on par with this woman. He needed to meet Javed and learn some trendy philosophies and cool buzzwords. He needed to figure out a way to manoeuvre Ajivikas into their conversations. Was he being overly hopeful, trying to impress a girl like Snigdha? Wasn't she really way out of his league? Was there anything in him that would attract a girl like her? 'Monkey balls,' he muttered, without realizing he had said it out loud.

She laughed, but this time, the laughter was muted by the auto as it slowed down to stop in front of them. Alice only dimly registered the bargaining and deliberations that ensued. Soon, Snigdha was in the auto waving him goodbye. He waved back.

On his way back, he became resistant to the cold. A warm feeling began to spread to his extremities outwards from his stomach. The silence of the night pounded mercilessly on his eardrums. The moon hid behind a cluster of clouds and the tree was now attached only to one dark shadow landlocked by the saffron-tinted road. The guard outside the ATM was asleep and his snores replaced the growls of the now absent bitch. At a distance, he could see Nitin, Iyengar and Bakchod waiting for him, probably eager to find out what he and Snigdha had talked about.

As he walked up to them, he could sense in himself that familiar mixture of irrepressible joy, a strange light-headedness, gut-wrenching nausea, hyperventilation and palm sweat. Yes, the symptoms were all there. He was beginning to fall for her.

4

Memento mori. Snigdha had set the bar pretty high, and although Alice felt pretty confident about topping it, it had been more than a week and he felt like he hadn't said a single smart thing to her. In their text-conversation the previous night, she had mentioned Friedrich Nietzsche in some context that Alice could no longer remember, but the fact that she mentioned the brooding German gave Alice direction. He went over to Javed's place and stayed back because Javed wouldn't let him borrow *Thus Spake Zarathustra*.

~

The phone had rung well after three o'clock just as Alice braced himself for a chapter called 'The Three Metamorphoses'. When Ananya's name flashed on his phone, he freaked out. And rightly so, he felt. Out-of-touch ex-girlfriends never call in the wee hours of the morning for anything good. Alice had let the phone ring about seven times and then picked up, although hesitantly.

'Hello…?'

'Listen, it's something really important, that's why I called so late,' she said hurriedly, without pausing for breath.

'Yeah, it's cool.' Yes, cool was good. Neutral. 'Tell me, what's up?' If 'what's up' wasn't casual, he didn't know what was.

'You remember Tanya, right?' Ananya asked.

'Tanya, who?' Alice asked, pretending like he was trying hard to remember.

'Tanya Dey. Who else? There was only one Tanya in college,' Ananya sounded irritated. He was extremely familiar with that tone.

'Right … it's really late and I… Anyway, what's up with her?' Alice felt stupid about pulling this drama for no reason; they weren't even dating, and she couldn't possibly know that he had thought of Tanya while making out with Ananya that one time. Or could she?

'I got a call from her landlady, because you know I visited her a couple of…' Ananya sounded scared and confused.

'Hey! Did something happen to Tanya?' Something inside Alice told him bad news was on its way.

'She hung herself from a fan in her apartment… Yeah, she was brought dead to the hospital. I think you should talk to Meera. I could call her, but I think she would prefer to hear from you because you both are so close.'

He had taken a couple of seconds to register what he had just been told. His first emotion had been that of a huge sense of relief. It wasn't something he had done. At once, though, he had felt ashamed of himself.

'Oh, fuck man! Um … I mean, this is a total shocker. Sad … um … tragic, yeah.' He had blinked twice and then let himself comprehend the implications of the news. 'Really nice of you to call and tell me,' he said, but not so genuinely.

'No problem. Just call Meera. I think someone should really be talking to her.'

'Yeah, sure.' Say bye before she does. Say it bitch! Say it! 'I'll call her now, bye.'

'Okay, bye.'

Yes! He had done it! First bye, baby! 'That's a win, right?' he had asked his brain. Someone died, you bastard, his brain had reprimanded. He sobered down immediately.

Tanya Dey was dead. One of the college hotties. Extremely introverted to a point where most girls thought she was a snob. Armed with a bubbling reservoir of enthusiasm coupled with selective and mercurial love, Meera was one of the very few people who had managed to become friends with her. Alice wanted to meet Meera very badly, just then, but Meera and Tanya were in Benares doing their masters. Well, not Tanya any more.

Before he could think of anything else, he had dialled Meera's number. He wouldn't have been able to call her otherwise. She had picked up after about five rings.

'Hello.' Husky and tremulous.

'Meera.'

A brief silence and then the sobs had begun. So, she had already heard. He had let her cry for a minute, a minute and a half; and while she wept, he had decided he didn't want to think about anything else. So, he just listened to her weep. Very intently. Her sobs, like a folk song, emerged from deep within her in rustic tones; brief interludes to accommodate a cough or a sneeze after which the pace would quicken and a bridge would emerge before returning to the original refrain. When the sobs had eventually subsided, she was gasping for breath.

And then she began to talk.

For a while she had just asked him questions, all of them rhetorical. He had wanted to say something soothing, but all he could manage was, 'No one knows why these things happen, Meera. They just do and we have to find the strength to face them, I guess.' That was practically a 'deal with it' speech. Good job, his brain had sneered.

Then she spoke about Tanya for a while. About how she had met her the day before and how they were supposed to meet again the day after. How they had been planning a trip to the ghats the next weekend. How she had received the news through a phone call from Tanya's neighbours. Alice had breathed easy, for at least the questions seemed to have subsided. But he had been wrong. Could some kind of youthful depression prompt someone to take their own life? Why hadn't Tanya thought of calling her, Meera, even once before taking that drastic a step? Didn't she consider her a good enough friend? Was Tanya's suicide somehow her fault? Other similar questions had followed. He couldn't think of any cogent answers to her questions, so he carefully avoided all of them with as much tact as he could muster. Most of the questions were rhetorical anyway and the others he just didn't want to deal with.

And then Meera had delivered her coup de grace. She asked, 'What do you think happens when you die? Is there more or is that it?'

Alice had been stumped. He wasn't very sure what he could say. Before his brain could filter it out, he said. 'You know what Dumbledore says to Harry at the end of the first book, right?' His comment had taken her unawares because she let out a high-pitched 'Ha!' of a laugh and then perhaps shocked at having allowed herself that laugh, began sobbing with greater vigour immediately.

About an hour and a half later, Meera had managed to dry-weep herself to oblivion during Alice's sleep-deprived and highly questionable monologue about how different cultures reacted to death. Once Alice had made sure that the sounds emanating from her end were snores and the story of Markandeya, the fucking boy-wonder, had reached its illogical end with the stubborn brat throwing a tantrum to avoid death itself, he disconnected the phone and wiggled his ear with a bedsheet-draped pinky to get rid of the sweat. For reasons beyond him, he walked into the loo, put some paste on his brush and began scrubbing his teeth.

As he watched the white foam of the toothpaste render his usually white teeth an unholy yellow, he felt that there was something horribly wrong with the whole concept of a twenty-two-year-old being dead. That, too, someone he knew closely. Wasn't death something that happened to old people with white hair or friends of friends, at worst?

A weird sense of disconnect began to take place within him like he had said his own name too many times and it had lost its meaning. He had dealt with death before, but only of older people who knew they would die; more importantly, he knew they would die. Tanya had converted the idea of death into a completely plausible reality. He began to feel uneasy like he had felt when he had attended a friend's wedding: a fist-clench in his gut that had been set off by the realization that a distant inevitability was swiftly turning into a very real possibility.

~

Javed woke up freakishly early even in winters. He was bathed, ready, and at the table eating his breakfast by the time Alice finally tumbled out of the room.

'You look like you saw a ghost,' smiled Javed.

'Good morning to you too,' spat Alice.

'What happened? Did somebody die?'

Alice looked up. 'Yeah, my friend Tanya, from college. She committed suicide.'

'Oh ... fuck! That almost never happens!' exclaimed Javed.

'What?'

'I asked you if someone died as a figure of speech, but somebody did actually die. The odds are insane if you think about it.'

'Well, maybe don't think about that. Instead think about the fact that a person died.'

'I know, I know. It's really sad. But the dead can't feel anything. So why feel sad for the dead?'

Ever since Javed's favourite uncle to whom Javed was very close had passed away, he often elicited brutal opinions on life and death. The event had traumatized him and therefore, he felt entitled to be a dick. It's not that Javed had not always been a dick. He was a bright and smart-mouthed kind of a dick. But the news of his uncle's death the previous year made his dickish humour grave. His obsession with ancient religions, too, definitely intensified in the last year.

Zubair and Ahmed were his two uncles and Alice wasn't sure which one had died. When Javed first told him it, he had neglected to mention which uncle it was and at that time it certainly wasn't a pertinent question to ask. However, as time went on, it became a literally impossible question to ask. Subsequently, Alice just hoped that eventually the other one would also die and then he'd find out who was who.

'The dead are finally at peace. The real tragedy is the survivor's,' mused Javed.

'Yeah, Meera has taken it pretty badly,' said Alice. He didn't feel like talking to Javed about this. He wanted to focus on the lovely omelettes Chhotu had made so that he could forget about the whole sordid business. He added more pepper to the one on his plate and then added a generous sprinkling directly into the tomato ketchup.

'So how did you like the book?' asked Javed.

'I read one chapter. It was nice, I guess.'

'One chapter? That's all?'

'It was really boring. I was sort of waiting for the philosophy part which never came.'

'You'll have to read the story. The story is *about* philosophy. It's allegorical.'

'Yeah, I felt it might be something pretentious like that,' said Alice. 'Anyway, I've decided to read the summary and reviews online, and just fake it. I've seen the book cover, read a few pages too. The little bits I know can be the nuggets of fact that I wrap my bullshit around.'

'Why do you like this girl so much?'

'She's cute and she reads books and knows cool philosophy. That's like everything I want in a girl. Also, she seems like a nice person. Added bonus.' Alice finished his omelette and got to work on the cold kheer from last night.

'Enlightenment-age philosophy is not cool. It's a philosophy for phonies.'

'You said this was one of your favourite books.'

'Yeah, but that was way back… Oh, right. She's your age. Well, fine, have your little fun with enlightenment, kids, but be sure to grow out of it.'

Alice felt like he just had a brainwave. 'Javed! Why don't you tell me something really cool about the Ajivika philosophy? Not something boring like what you would find cool. Tell me something that's actually cool.'

Javed scratched his chin. 'I think in Valmiki's Ramayana, Ravana is in disguise as an Ajivika when he comes to abduct Sita. That's pretty interesting, right?'

Alice held his face in his hand. 'That's exactly the kind of lame thing only you'd find interesting. How am I supposed to bring up Ravana in conversation out of nowhere? I have to be as good-looking as Bakchod if I want to do shit like that and still have girls fall for me.'

Javed clucked dismissively. 'Fuck off then. I don't know what you want to hear. I can't make up interesting stuff for your benefit.'

'I am sure there's something interesting. Like, why do people think that the religion stretches back to the Indus Valley?' Alice asked and then wagged his right eyebrow for effect.

'You know what, that's a great question. There are several ... what *you'd* call ... boring reasons. But there's also this. Ajivikas believed in a kind of determinism. They believed that everything that happened was the result of a web of three interconnecting factors: Niyati, Sangati and Bhava. This concept has parallels across the ancient world. The bronze age Mesopotamians had fate goddesses and the Iron age Greeks had them too and exactly three in number, called the three Moirai. Similar ideas can be found in Egypt, Persia and early Vedic India. So historians conjecture that such a concept might have had very ancient origins. Since we know nothing about the Indus Valley Civilisation, its tempting to imagine that is where these ideas came from. And also impossible to disprove. That's the more important thing.

'This is definitely as good as memento mori. And what's more, it's not Latin or something. It's really local. "*Saare jahaan se achcha, Hindustan hamara,*" So what do those words mean? Neeti, Basha and ... what? What's the third one?'

'Okay, focus. Don't fuck this up. Write it down if you have to. Niyati. Niyati is justice. Sangati. Sangati is serendipity. And Bhava is svabhava or the subject and object's innate natures. These are the three factors whose interaction determines our fate, according to the Ajivikas.'

Alice took his phone out and typed the words as a message back to Javed. 'Niyati, Sangati and Svabhava ...

Okay. Now I just need to figure out how to bring this up in conversation.'

~

Alice didn't usually go to his office until noon, so he stopped by to drink his morning chai with Nitin and Bakchod. He didn't really want to, but Bakchod was adamant. 'What kind of a friend are you?' he had cried when he called Alice. 'Nitin's leaving in less than a week!' Nitin was leaving in ten days.

'Sure, but Suttah Point is out of my way. You just come to Yash's stall.' Bakchod usually asked Nitin to bring Iyengar along for their periodic communal breakfasts, but Nitin never woke her up too early. When asked why, he quoted the Hogwarts motto. That was another in Alice's list of 'cool Latin phrases': Draco dormiens nunquam titillandus. Never tickle a sleeping dragon. That was the first entry in a page that had only five entries. Alice had added the last one a few weeks earlier. Memento mori. Live in awareness of death.

Nitin was already there sitting cross-legged on the platform looking like a village thug with his dark eyes, hook nose and Liam Neeson-as-Ra's-al-Ghul-goatee on a broader jaw. Underneath the jaw was a dark, coarse but tastefully woven shawl, out of the folds of which one of his hands jutted out holding a glass of cutting chai. When they sat down next to him, he placed his free hand on Alice's shoulder in an avuncular manner and said, 'I really, really hope you are going to work at least today.' Alice jerked his other shoulder to indicate the bag on his back. 'I am going to office today because I have to get out of the house anyway to meet Snigdha for lunch. Somehow, getting out of the house and still not going to work seemed like a deliberate karma-provoker.'

'Since when have you started worrying about karma?' laughed Nitin.

'Since Bakchod started chanting verses from the Gita every morning, I have been forced to ponder not just the material consequences of my actions, but the karmic ones as well. So, what does our good book say on the subject, Bakchod?'

Bakchod shot back, 'The Bhagavad Gita says, "Do your job, asshole; even if you want to chase panties during lunch, go back, finish the work, and make sure you don't get fired. The rent shalt not pay itself, Arjuna."'

'But I do want to get fired, man. I don't want to do this kind of work.'

Bakchod put his negotiating voice on. 'But you don't know what you want to do either. So just keep doing this job to pay the bills while you figure that out.'

'No, but I don't want to do anything. I just want to hang out with Snigdha throughout the day and then with you guys after work,' sighed Alice. 'I wish I were born rich.'

'It's "was" not "were",' cried Bakchod triumphantly. 'You keep correcting my grammar. How does it feel now?'

Before Alice could correct him, Yash, the chaiwallah, passed them their chais and biscuits, and Alice's stomach had already started groaning, making noises that one would find while heavy machinery was being run in factories.

'You've brought the chai just as I was about to pass out from fatigue,' cried Bakchod, beaming at the food and at Yash. Then, placing the chai in front of him and the biscuit balanced on top of it, he slapped his thigh and rubbed his hands together, following these gestures with dipping the biscuit into the smoking hot chai, pulling it out and, while it was still fecund with the brown liquid that was dripping from it, he put it in his mouth, warning Nitin and Alice with a grimace on his face that the chai was still too hot.

On the other side of the platform on which they were sat was a huge building with car parking, ATMs, and even a bar they frequented. The building was somehow important, but in the four years Alice had been around, he had never cared to find out what it was. The ignorance had become a secret game to be relished; one of many he played, sometimes in isolation and sometimes in companionship: like how neither he nor Meera had ever entered their college store that was inaugurated in their first year, or like the Delhi Fashion Week that Biswas and he managed to avoid four years in a row, managing assignments through 'jugaad' and second-hand information. The large, open space in front of the building was home to a hundred or so Bihari migrants who lived there in the open, alone or as families, under sunshades or trees, outside ATM machines, in uniform destitution and cheer. A lucky few who could forge a bond that made them seem like brothers sharing the same bloodline with the owner of Suttah Point or Yash found employment in one of the several franchises they set up ever since they landed there, not unlike like these people, some forty-odd years ago as teenage flunkies. The not-so-lucky others went into construction or perhaps even joined the organized begging mafia. They owned the front veranda of this office building in an anarchist, you-have-it-and-I-need-it kind of a way. Alice liked to think of it as street-side communism. The kids begged, at first coyly and then with mawkish abandon, while the toddlers rode on dogs.

'I can't believe you'll get to eat cheap and lovely Udupi dosas every single day. And idlis,' said Bakchod, a wistful look in his eyes and a faraway grin on his face.

'One gets used to these things very quickly,' countered Alice. 'I pretty much pissed my pants with excitement at the thought that I would get to eat chapatis every day when I found out I was coming here for college. Now you couldn't pay me to eat fucking wheat. Speaking of which, dinner at your place tonight?' he asked Nitin.

'Fine. Just get capsicum, tomato and aloo when you come home.'

~

Alice mooched around in a quasi-comfortable revolving chair waiting for the seconds to tick by in the western corner of his large office, which housed nearly thirty employees. These moments, when he was not distracted by something he had to do, had a tendency to wrap themselves around him, threatening to never leave. He had finished whatever little work had come by his way that morning; his irregularity ensured he was not a central part of any assignment. In an organization with less than thirty members, only interns and employees serving out their notices were not involved centrally in any project at all. He should have been worried about his situation in the office, but Alice was not.

He had called Snigdha about fifteen minutes earlier, almost ready to get out of the office. She made him sit back down citing some important work that had landed itself on her desk. Fifteen minutes max, she had promised.

With nothing to do, Alice placed the phone on his desk, and touching either side of his skull at the temples with his index fingers, began to will the phone to ring with the sheer power of his mind. He was finding the exercise in telekinesis rather engaging, while the accounts manager and, a member of the technical staff who usually asserted their professional independence by not interacting with the designers in any way, walked past behind him and out of the door to hop on to their Bajaj something-or-the-other and zoom away to some restaurant.

Alice turned his left index finger about forty-five degrees, fixed his other index finger a little more firmly on the temple, lifted his pinky up, gritted his teeth and grunted so loudly that it startled the office boy; it was also then that the phone rang and startled Alice no less. Alice, pleased with his effort and flushed with success, picked the phone up on the third ring.

'Hi, I made you call with the power of my mind.'

'Fascinating. Can you also finish my work with the power of your mind? Because I don't think I can come out for lunch now.'

'Damn! If you had told me a minute earlier, I could have slinked off with Mr Sharma and the IT sextet to Rajinder Dhaba for lunch where we would have discussed the latest game-changing tweak in Windows Whatever.'

'They sound lovely.'

'They watch YouTube videos of Bill Gates' speeches, Windows launches, and blooper reels of these speeches and launches...'

'I weep for you over your missed opportunity, but I have to go now. As compensation, though, how 'bout we meet early and I stay for dinner?'

'Wow! Mighty presumptuous of you to assume that your staying for dinner works as compensation for me. Vanity, thy name is... No, no, woman, thy name is... Shit ... I forgot whose name is what...'

'I'll take that to mean: sure, let's meet at five. Bye,' she said and hung up.

~

Since lunch was delayed, Alice decided to go back to trying to figure out how to bring the Ajivikas up in conversation with Snigdha. He tried out various combinations with all the information and the names he had. They threw up a few interesting results. Having read those for a while, when he realized that the next several links were PDFs of historians' research theses, he decided to skip those and jumped ahead to the fourth page where he found a website: the 'temple of Ajivikism'. He clicked on the link, and it took him to a basic HTML website with a badly aligned Google image of the universe.

On the top, in big red letters, was the legend 'Niyati * Sangati * Bhava'.

Alice clicked on 'About' and some faintly legible letters appeared at the centre of the universe. It bore a description of the Ajivika cult as known from the same limited sources and was roughly an edited version of the Wikipedia page. He returned to the home page and scouted a little more. Andromeda, thereabouts, was a cluster of letters battling to be read against a bunch of meteorites. Upon inspection, he deciphered it to be 'Contact Us' and clicked on it.

If you want to join or have questions about this religion, please schedule a chat with the priest. Please submit your email and name and we shall intimate you regarding the details of the chat.

Alice was excited. He quickly filled in his details and clicked submit. Even though he knew it would probably be ages before he got any sort of reply, he kept checking for a reply all day, annoying even himself in the process. He knew he couldn't expect a pat reply, it was after all on the fourth page of the Google search and if he had been tech-savvy enough he would have probably found out when the last post had been posted and realized it was probably several years ago.

He had checked his mail at least once every day since then, expecting a reply.

Presently, Alice checked his mail again. Nothing. He started feeling restless. He logged on to his Orkut account. No activity except for someone who had thanked him and about fifty others for their prayers and blessings now that their grandfather was all right. He was tempted to reply 'welcome', but instead started to fantasize about getting fired. He slowly relished all the different ways in which he could provoke his boss into firing him. Deciding not to do anything drastic but to still do something, he got off his chair, walked up to his boss's cabin and started to pace around outside it to try. He meant to induce his boss into saying something. Anything. About his constant absenteeism, his lack of interest in projects, his hair.

After about five minutes he saw motion behind the frosted glass and the door opened slightly from behind which emerged an eye, a glass, a nose, a cheek and two chins. 'Can you come in here for a sec? No, actually, I'll come out there.' The rest of him emerged six-foot-tall, with two eyes, two hands, two legs, shirt, trousers and a blazer.

Ha! Alice's brain cried in triumph. At last we shall tell His Majesty what we think of him.

'I have noticed that you haven't been bringing the whole one hundred per cent of yourself to work over the last few weeks. But it's okay. Don't worry, champ. I was once like you too. We all have our burnouts. But this is a start-up, and everyone has to step in, so I think you've had a good break. Now get back in full and swinging, huh.'

Alice groaned inwardly.

'What say, champ? Are we back in and ready to go? The full two hundred per cent?'

'Yeah, yes, of course. Thanks for the talk. Cool,' replied Alice, defeated. He couldn't build up a rant when the other person was being all positive and rainbows out of his ass. Sly, blazer-wearing bastard, his brained screamed. Coward! Pussy! Peter Pettigrew!

~

The nickel-toothed old man sitting at one of the tables outdoors at Barista had probably smiled at Alice and Snigdha with empathy at their decision to sit outside in the cold to avoid the football match that was being telecast inside. Manchester United vs Barcelona, Alice had guessed wildly without betraying any apprehension and Snigdha, nodding brightly, had agreed probably because disagreement would have involved finding out who was actually playing. The withered winter sun had slipped out of sight, but the sky retained a gaudy orange; this gave the illusion of warmth tricking them into sitting outside.

They had, on their first one-on-one dinner, tried to figure out where a particularly odd couple had come from (socio-culturally, Snigdha had asked), and both had found the exercise to be so engaging that they started to do it for everybody. Alice took the game to the next level by insisting they closely observe the subjects and then make inferences about them, also explaining their inferences which would have to be agreed to by the opposite party. And the mutually agreed policy was to be lenient towards sweeping generalizations and dubious anthropological theories, either condemned or concocted. Snigdha had christened the activity 'Aatreya', because it was her favourite name. 'Favourite name for what?' Alice had asked, certain that 'Aatreya' was a stupid name for a made-up gamish, time-passish thingamajiggy. 'Generally favourite name. I like the way it sounds. If I had to name something something, I would name it whatever my favourite name was. That's what a favourite name is.' That settled, the incongruous name had stuck.

Alice wasn't hungry; neither was he interested in ordering something in an overpriced café. Sitting outside further shielded them from the need to order. And so, Alice was happy. He pulled out a crumpled-up pack of cigarettes from his torn jeans, noticing that the portion of exposed thigh from the tear had become almost blue from the cold. He lit the cigarette, but Snigdha snatched it out of his hands and put it out. He was slightly taken aback for it was not like her at all to object to his smoking or any of his other habits at all. She stubbed it out, half-heartedly, in the ashtray and reached for her backpack. After much excavation—during which a lot of artifacts such as a mobile phone, a piece of sandalwood wrapped in a paper, a lighter, and a white napkin with plastic packing, which might have been a sanitary pad, came out—she pulled out a fat, crumpled, hand-rolled joint. Stubbing the cigarette out properly, Alice said, 'I think we should wait for that guy who snorts that stuff with that aluminum foil thing.' Picking the lighter up and busting the joint, she said through pursed lips, 'He is already snorting behind you. Came in just now and got down to business.'

She took a long drag and blew out the smoke extravagantly. 'I told Jeevan you are a pot lover, so he rolled us a joint of the best Idukki gold.'

'Wow! Thank Jiva profusely on my behalf! Tell him he is a gentleman, a scholar and an emerald amongst random stones.'

'Jeevan!'

'Oh, sorry! Jeevan. Thank him.'

'But don't you know Jeevan? I talk about him all the time.'

'No, you don't.'

'Yes, I do! My best friend, the love of my life Jeevan, who I would have married except that he fell in love with the awesomest girl in the whole wide world and got married to her.' She gasped in a weird voice whilst holding the smoke in. She finally blew the smoke out and passed the joint to Alice.

Alice took it and while examining and sniffing it, said, 'Hmm … yeah, sounds familiar… Yes, I think you told me about this guy. Listen, do you really want to get munchies in Barista?'

'No, we'll go somewhere after. Suttah Point maybe.'

They smoked slowly, talking intermittently while watching the metro outside Alice's college in construction, and playing Aatreya, during which time the joint went out several times. When it went out for the fifth time, they lost interest in relighting it and rats were gnawing at the insides of Alice's stomach. However, Snigdha was too stoned to move and so, insisted on continuing with the game.

The man in the hot seat was the nickel-toothed old man. Based on his strong arms, a beret cap and an erect back, Alice managed to establish an uncontested army background. The plastic grocery bag with the logo helped Snigdha establish his whereabouts within a radius of a kilometre of Aurobindo Marg. Again uncontested. Alice then tried to insist that the man was a widower or a divorcee since he did not have a ring on his fingers. Snigdha contested this statement vehemently and called Alice a 'city slicker far too influenced by western sitcoms'.

'Well, so are you,' answered Alice indignantly.

'That's true. Sorry for taking off on you. I think it's the munchies.'

'Let's go.'

They exited and after crossing the junction, Alice bought her a paper cone of hot, tasty pakodas with radish salad and ate most of the pakodas himself. Unlike the pakodas back home that were large and looked like hairy bugs, these were small, yellow and shaped like testicles. He then apologized verbally with a full mouth, offered to buy Snigdha another cone, realized he didn't have any more money, sheepishly borrowed the money from her, bought her another cone and this time, decently, only ate about three of them.

By the time they began to walk towards Suttah Point, it was already dark. The roads were thick with office-to-home traffic. Snigdha decided to clean her spectacles, which turned out to be an intensive and long-drawn out exercise, so they walked in silence for a while.

At eight in the night Suttah Point was, as usual, abustle with activity. In their usual perch were Nitin, Ravi, Kaamya and Vikram, who was obscuring the familiar scene of Iyengar and Bakchod bickering over a foiled prank.

'The beer has been waiting for you guys for so long!' scolded Bakchod, spotting Alice and Snigdha on the other side of the road.

''Whoh!' No beer for me,' shouted Snigdha while crossing, 'I am rather stoned.'

'So what? That is that and this is this,' slurred Bakchod, slapping Alice on the back and handing him a beer. Alice declined and pointed to his blown eyes. Bakchod, however, was not in a mood to relent and began to take it upon himself to convince Alice. 'You need to enter God Mode today, man' was the refrain after each reason was cited.

Finally, when Alice realized Bakchod was not going to stop anytime soon, and had actually managed to whip up some support from others, even Snigdha, he gave up and said, 'Okay, please enter the cheat code.'

Bakchod cried in triumph and shouted out the letters 'M-P-K-F-A' while pressing imaginary keys on Alice's nose. 'God Mode is on.'

Alice took the can of beer, chugged it down while slightly worrying about how easy it had become for him to chug a whole can of strong beer, then crushed it, flung it on the ground and roared, 'MAGIC CLAW!' while the others cheered and clapped encouragingly.

For the next couple of hours followed routine debauchery, inside jokes and work stories. Aided by the joint he had smoked, Alice was soon uncontrollably high and just sat on the stone next to Snigdha smiling at everyone amicably. He then managed to convince Snigdha to share a beer with him, after which she even put a hand around his shoulder. Soon he was inches away from passing out and everyone else had gotten to that weird point in drunkenness where they would ardently apologize and forgive each other for past sins, real and imagined. So, Alice announced that he would be tottering back home to crash. Bakchod wanted to stay on, so he started to walk alone, but Snigdha suddenly said, 'I'll make sure he reaches safely,' and started to walk with him.

The walk back to his apartment was comfortably silent. Neither of them talked but walked quietly step in step. Every once in a while, their fingers would brush, sending his arms into shocks of ecstasy, making him wonder if he should reach out for her hand and hold it only to wuss out immediately. Once or twice he even thought he saw Snigdha smile when it happened, but he knew he was way too high to do or say anything at all that he would not later regret. Unlike others who did stupid things when drunk, Alice felt his guard was at its strongest when he was drunk. In the four years of college, he was probably the only one in the entire student populace who had not drunk-called, drunk-kissed or drunk-fucked.

Once they reached his flat, he thought Snigdha would leave, but she helped him remove the grill, get in, and then got him to help her get in. Once they were inside, Alice fell on the mattress. In whispers and gestures, he asked her to get the sleeping bag and zip him up in it. Chuckling to herself and saying something he could not understand, she went about the task and actually managed to accomplish it in good time and also covered his ears and neck with a muffler. His face was only about a foot away from hers but it was getting increasingly blurred. 'Fanks, Wigda,' he mumbled, slightly out of panic. Her out-of-focus face broke into a smile and started to approach his own slowly but steadily. The face got more and more blurred, and he felt her fingers tuck the muffler under his chin, exposing his nose and mouth. He sensed her lips against his.

And then there was bliss extending from one eternity to the next. The intensity of his joy knocked the socks off his brain, making him pass out almost immediately.

5

Alice was not sure if he had woken up. His head felt a little heavy and his vision was still populated by the items he had seen in his dream. A brown table impeccably laid out with silverware and a lone full cup of Black Forest Fantasy ice cream half melted and dripping from the sides. The transition from dream to waking was taking an unusually long time. He tried to move his legs and felt something warm and wet on his thighs. He was jolted into wakefulness.

Had he just come in his pants while having a dream about a Black Forest Fantasy ice cream? His fingers dove into the sleeping bag to investigate. They confirmed the worst. He shook his head while trying to comprehend what had just happened. He had involuntarily jerked off to an ice cream. What on Freudian earth could that possibly mean?

He extracted himself from the sleeping bag and checked it thoroughly. Fortunately, the bag hadn't been stained. Genuine Jockey had borne the brunt of it valiantly. Walking with bowed legs he made his way slowly to the loo and switched the geyser on. This geyser was one of those tiny ones that heated the water quickly; but it also needed to be kept switched on through the duration of the shower, increasing risk of electrocution.

He prolonged the process of removing his clothes to give time for the water to heat. Passed out in all four layers for the second time this month, his brain observed grimly. He removed three layers of upper clothing with his pelvis thrust slightly inwards to minimize the seepage on to his jeans. Then he gingerly peeled the jeans off his legs. By the time he removed his underwear, threw it into the bucket and let the water run, the water had heated sufficiently. He closed the tap and turned the shower on.

Alice melted away under the force of the water. His brain, which felt like mush, seemed to respond only when the full force of the water from the shower was on his skull. He used his fingers to wade through his pubic hair and make a thorough job of the cleaning. You can't simply wash away what happened, his brain sniggered.

After changing into fresh clothes (fresh did not indicate absolute freshness, but merely that they weren't the very same that had just been cast out), he called Bakchod. It rang fifteen times before Bakchod picked up.

'Hi hero. So … tell me.'

'What?' asked Alice, wondering what Bakchod knew about the previous night.

'What, what?' asked Bakchod.

'What, what what? What are you talking about?' barked Alice irritated.

'Well … spit it out,' sang Bakchod.

'Spit what out?' Alice asked cautiously.

'What happened last night?'

'Nothing,' said Alice.

'Hmmm … very suspicious.'

'What's suspicious?'

'Snigdha said the exact same thing.'

'So?'

'That's exactly what you guys would say if something happened.'

'But that's also exactly what we would say if nothing happened.'

'There is that problem…' admitted Bakchod. 'So you just passed out and she came back?'

'Yeah. Are you at Nitin's?'

'We all are?'

'Snigdha is there too?' Alice couldn't keep the shock out of his voice.

'Oh my god! Something definitely happened,' yelped Bakchod.

'Shhhhh … stop yelling. Nothing happened okay. So please don't make it weird. Just come down for chai. I'll talk to you.'

There were some noises in the background. 'Oye, Nitin is up. Meet us at Yash's in half an hour, I'll wake the others,' said Bakchod quickly.

'Surely not Iyengar too?!'

'If she tries to punch me, I'll tackle her. I have been watching all those martial arts videos to prepare myself for this very moment. When you make your mind your fortress, bodily defence is simply a matter of…'

Alice cut the call.

~

Yash was especially talkative that morning and since the others hadn't come yet and an urchin was pestering him for change, Alice sat on a ledge and engaged him in conversation with equal enthusiasm. Defeated, the urchin too sat on the ledge next to Alice, listening intently to their conversation and even giggling and snorting with abandon whenever he wished. The road was empty except for parked vehicles. It was a holiday and not too many people were out. A pleasant mist hung about, occasionally sliced by the sunlight, but in a soft, graceful sort of way. The conversation was light. Movies and matches.

After a while, Yash's anecdotes began to get a little biographical. 'I've done my shit in life, you know. Raised two sons. Both married. Both living abroad. They even ask me to come live with them, but I don't want to. Independence is very important to me. Unlike others I don't even ask them to send any money home. My stall and my newspapers.' He waved his hand over the items.

Alice hoped what Yash was saying about his situation was true. As a kid, the time he came back home from school and sat for lunch was the time for the matinee movie on the cable channel. His grandparents watched it without fail, and he sat and watched the movies with them. They were unfailingly melodramatic with plots or at least prominent subplots dedicated to describing the atrocities committed by a young couple towards either party's progenitors. They would either stay with their parents and ill-treat them, or move out leaving them behind in abject poverty or some such horror. But Yash was reputed to earn a lot from the shop.

Still, at his age, it wouldn't be about the money. What did he think of not being able to see his grandchildren grow up? Alice didn't really want to ask. He liked to talk to Yash about politics. He liked to talk to people who didn't have that typical, tiring, middle-class cynicism about politics. Unlike the so-called educated middle classes, working class people actually understood politics because they were forced to live with the political consequences of their vote. He felt that middle-class people generally loved thinking politics was dirty or that it doesn't bring change because it exempted them from thinking deeply about something as complex as society and they had enough money that they didn't have to depend on welfare. So, even the smartest people only seemed up to the challenge of de-politicized philosophy or, if desperate to appear smart, maybe quantum physics or something like that. Maybe that's what Javed had meant about enlightenment philosophy too: the idea that enlightenment was an individualistic issue and not a socio-political problem. That we need to solve the problem of the empty stomach before attempting to empty the mind.

Very few people took real joy in wading through the murky waters of social politics and grappling with the real big questions of caste or labour, not fake, pointless ones like how was the universe created or what happens when you bombard quarks with some other piece of shit. Yash campaigned for political parties or independent candidates in various elections, especially the municipal level ones. He had also campaigned to legalize buildings in several portions of the colony that Nitin and Iyengar lived in.

Bakchod arrived shortly, bellowing exuberant greetings at Alice and Yash. He slapped Alice on the shoulder, shooed the urchin away with intimidating gestures and sat down.

'Yashji, chai and two biscuits. What were you guys talking about?'

'Where are the others?' Alice asked, cutting Yash off before he could answer.

'Your love is arriving shortly, my man. Don't be so impatient.' Bakchod grinned and sat in the spot left empty by the urchin.

'Why did you come ahead?' asked Alice in English. Yash began to rearrange his cups.

'Nitin and Snigdha are calming Iyengar down and once she is not psycho anymore, they'll come.'

'Did you really splash water on her?'

'Plausible deniability. Their roof is always leaking.'

'Why do you do this shit, man?'

'Because it works. Bottom line is, she is coming for chai.'

'How do you know? She might go back to sleep.'

'Ha! She wishes. She kept screaming, "I can't even go back to sleep, you bastard" again and again. So she'll have to come. Just you see.' He turned to Yash. 'Sorry, you were saying…'

'Nothing important,' Yash said and then leaned in. 'I heard a girl from your college committed suicide.'

Alice looked at Bakchod to see if he knew.

Bakchod scowled. 'Yashji, it's true. Very sad. But that's all we had been talking about yesterday. Enough. Let's talk about happy things.' He turned to Alice. 'So … spit it out. What happened?'

Alice took a deep breath and sighed. 'I don't know really. I was very drunk. I don't want to say anything before talking to her.'

'Please don't tell me you guys had sex because she came back pretty soon. I expect better from you.'

'Shut up, fucker. We might or might not have kissed. That's all.'

'You either kissed or you didn't. There's not a lot of grey area there.' Bakchod chuckled.

'I was drunk.'

'So you tried to kiss her and she knocked you out with a blunt object?'

'Whoa, is that what happened?' cried Alice, panicking. 'I really hope not. I remember it quite differently.'

'So how do you remember it? Let's go through the events.' Yash handed Bakchod his chai.

'There's not a lot of events to go through. We went up to our room and then I remember her putting a blanket over me. And then she leaned in and kissed me I think.'

Bakchod raised his eyebrows and looked at Alice. And then he burst out laughing. 'So she tucked you into bed and then kissed you. Man. That's really fucked up.'

'Shut up, asshole. She didn't tuck me in. She put a blanket on me. It was really hot and steamy and totally … like … awesome and not at all weird.'

Bakchod continued to laugh, but he also slapped Alice on the back and shook his hand. They finished their chais as Bakchod chatted with Yash about the Bhagavad Gita in the context of Tanya's death.

Alice wondered what to do when Snigdha eventually came down for chai. Should he catch her eye and give her some kind of look that said, I remember what happened, let's talk later? But what would that look be like? What if he accidentally gave her a look that said, what have you done, you immoral woman? It is probably best if you avoid her eye altogether and wait for an opportunity to talk to her alone, his brain suggested.

Nitin, Snigdha and Iyengar turned up a good fifteen minutes later, looking dishevelled and sleepy. Alice snuck looks at Snigdha to see if he could draw her attention, but she seemed to resolutely look anywhere but his way. Since Alice could see them from down the road, they seemed to take forever to get there, allowing Alice enough time to feel hopeful, worry, give up in exhaustion and worry again about how the morning would play out.

Finally, when they sat on the wall, it was five people in a row. So as the tacit code demanded, Alice and Bakchod got up and stood in front of the others, forming a circle for ease of conversation.

'You! Out of my view,' yelled Iyengar at Bakchod. He giggled but he also moved away. Snigdha looked pretty in that awesome sleepy way. Puffy eyes. Loose T-shirt. Hastily drawn ponytail. Glasses slightly askew. And this girl had kissed him last night. The universe has some sense of humour, his brain laughed. But hey! As long as it's laughing with us and not at us, right?

'How's Meera doing?' Nitin asked Alice while blowing the steam off his chai.

'Yeah, is she okay?' Iyengar enquired, her angry, sleepy face rearranging itself in concern.

'Yeah, she is fine,' Alice responded automatically and then corrected himself. 'Actually, I don't think she is. She was pretty shaken last morning. I've been texting her but her replies don't seem encouraging.'

'Were Tanya and Meera very close?' asked Snigdha.

Alice took the opportunity to looked searchingly at Snigdha's face. Why wasn't she giving anything away?

'They were roommates. She was one of Tanya's few close friends,' Nitin answered.

'Not that Tanya was asocial,' asserted Iyengar. 'I thought she was just reserved. I really liked her for it. Normally these pretty model-types can never shut up.'

'Do we really have to talk about this?' grumbled Bakchod. 'It's like there has been nothing else to talk about since yesterday morning.'

'We were partying last night,' countered Alice.

'Yeah, but we started to drink because we were sad about her. And then we thought we should just celebrate her life instead, because we got drunk pretty early.' Bakchod took more biscuits from the bottle on Yash's cart counter.

'So, what's our plan after this?' asked Iyengar.

'Lunch, of course. Wherever Nitin wants to go.'

'I've got to go pack,' said Nitin.

'You can pack later,' Bakchod waved his hand nonchalantly.

'I really have a lot of packing to do.'

'We'll have an early lunch.'

'I just really want to go home,' said Snigdha.

'Me too,' said Alice quickly. They all looked at Iyengar.

'I actually wouldn't mind lunch,' shrugged Iyengar.

Bakchod cried out in triumph. 'That's it. It's settled, we are going for lunch.'

'How's it settled?' asked Alice. 'It's three of us against two of you.'

'Yeah, but I could have taken on all four of you and convinced you. Now it's just three and I have Iyengar on my side. Why don't you guys just surrender? Resistance is futile.'

So they spent the next half an hour debating where they would go to eat, because although Bakchod said he would let Nitin pick, he kept vetoing any place anyone wanted to go to and no one wanted to go to any of the three places he had suggested. Finally, they settled on a restaurant that was the least objectionable to all parties so that everyone was equally dissatisfied.

~

Alice and Snigdha got some time alone with each other only after lunch. Snigdha said she had to go back home, and Alice walked out with her to see her off. In moments of stress, Alice liked to think of whatever was happening to him as a particular plot twist in the sitcom drama that was his life. Perhaps it was a way of externalizing the trauma or a way to cut the tension of the moment and try to get a third-person perspective on the whole thing.

While walking alongside Snigdha, he began to think of the last few months. It was a decent premise for an ensemble sitcom. Single guy in the city grappling with adulthood alongside friends who foster him and work as support mechanisms. Enter: girl of his dreams. It's obvious they are supposed to end up together, but what the script writers really cash in on is the 'will they, won't they'. It's a routine act, but the audience lap it up. Typically, obstacles are added to delay the inevitable and prolong the drama, but Alice had had enough. He felt there was no moment better than this. He decided this was more like a mini-series and the climax was close by.

Now that he had that sorted, he wondered what exactly to say. Snigdha seemed to be lost in thought too. They walked out of the gate and down the road in silence, before Alice got exhausted of running all the options in his head and just said, 'Snigdha, about last night…'

She immediately looked at him and said, 'I am really sorry about that. I was super-drunk. I didn't know what I was doing.'

'Are you sure? Because it was amazing,' replied Alice hurriedly. 'I know I passed out, but I shouldn't have mixed alcohol and weed. That's the only reason.'

'Really? You aren't just saying that?'

'What? Why would I just say that?' asked Alice indignantly. 'This is important stuff. It's not the sort of thing one would just say.'

Snigdha smiled. 'So it was good?'

'It knocked me out, Snigdha. What more can I say?'

She laughed but didn't say anything else. They walked in silence for a while longer but when they reached the main road, she climbed on to the footpath and walked away from the auto stand. The afternoon was cold but sunny. Alice took his sweater off and tied it around his waist. After a while she took his hand in hers and so, he panicked and said, 'Let me be honest... I sweat from my palms when it's cold and when I am nervous. And I am really both right now.' He expected her to recoil and pull her hand away. But she just chuckled and said, 'I'll hold it till it gets sweaty.'

'Cool. Yeah. You don't have to be polite or anything okay...'

'It's fine, Alice. Can we just walk?'

They walked down the road looking in different directions but smiling to themselves. Their joy found expression in just being with each other; nothing needed to be said. The guy who sold badam shake was back with his cart. Strangely enough he had taken Ananya to the same guy on the day they had started going steady. Snigdha drank the badam shake and complained that it had only cashews and so couldn't be called a badam shake.

They took the left opposite the kulfi cart and walked deep into the colony, past the area where the students lived. The houses hugged each other tightly in places and, in others, they poured into each other. The sides of the narrow road were choked with an unending array of cars into whose gaps countless bicycles, scooters and motorbikes were squeezed in impossible ways. They walked quietly in the middle of the road, pausing on the sides to let the occasional vehicle pass. Alice finally gathered the courage to ask her.

'Hey, Snigdha … so what does this mean?'

'I don't know … what do you think?' She didn't look at him, but her grip tightened slightly.

'Are we … like … maybe … going out?' Alice tried to make it sound like a suggestion.

'Hmmm … yeah. That would be nice. But what does that mean, really?'

'It means we can kiss when we aren't drunk, hopefully.'

'Yeah, that sounds nice. I am really looking forward to it.'

'Okay, but don't be so sure. I probably suck at kissing.'

'Haha. You were good yesterday.'

'I was drunk. I didn't know what I was doing. Total fluke.' Now that they had agreed to start going out, Alice felt the time for posturing was over and that they needed to prepare each other with the truth. There was a feeling of elation, but he tried to put it aside. Things needed to be clarified.

Snigdha, on the other hand, seemed totally at ease with him. She locked her arm into his and led him back to the main road. Most of the cars were covered in a sludge of dust and dew but somehow that day they looked beautiful to Alice. And the stench from the giant open drain nearby didn't seem as offending. All the clichés were coming true.

'So does this mean I start telling people I have a boyfriend?' Snigdha asked.

Alice grinned. 'I think it's important that you do. Especially to other guys.'

'And you'll tell people you have a girlfriend?'

'They won't believe me. So make sure you are around a lot.'

She laughed and hugged his arm tighter. On their entire walk back to Nitin and Iyengar's, Alice felt everything was surreal. He had wanted this so badly he had started to believe it would never happen and now that it had, he would really take some time to get used to the feeling of something finally going his way.

When they went back to Nitin and Iyengar's, there was a lot of screaming and hugging and high-fives going around. Bakchod produced a bottle of non-alcoholic champagne that had been lying around for months and sprayed it around, ruining Iyengar's Kalamkari bed sheets, but her mood couldn't be dampened. As his oldest friend in college, she took Alice's single status as a personal affront and she was smugly happy that he was with someone she had effectively set up. She wasn't going to let Bakchod get to her or ruin her day. She patted Bakchod on the shoulder and smiled, 'It's okay, I'll murder you some other day. In your sleep. I am saving this bottle so I can break it over your head and then stab you with it.'

~

Over the next few days, Alice got a sense that his sitcom drama had indeed reached a climax. The coming of age was perhaps complete after all. He hadn't figured everything out but that wasn't important. He had a job, a girlfriend, and a very, very uncertain future, but a future that he was looking forward to. He still didn't know what he wanted to do with his life, but the idea of figuring it out with Snigdha by his side charmed him.

His work seemed much more tolerable because it afforded him time to spend with Snigdha without worrying about money. And it was during the time she was busy too. So they were able to work out their schedules perfectly to spend as much time together as possible, eagerly catching up on the small and large details of each other's lives, the kind that would have bored anyone else into tearing their hair out, but they were in a place where they couldn't have enough of it and even demanded more details.

The ending of the series slackened and dragged out but it was a total fan-favourite. The characters had all come into their own and fit perfectly into each other like a jigsaw. The jokes were familiar but were gaining more finesse. Over the next few months, Alice settled into a routine with Snigdha. They spent most of their free time together, either by themselves or with Bakchod and Iyengar. For all of those months, routine ceased to seem dronish. Even the smallest moments had great significance. There were a lot of firsts and then there were double dates with friends whom he had lost touch with because they were couples.

Alice and Snigdha fought often about little things, but the fights were too charming to be remembered. And there was a lot of patch-up action to look forward to. They argued but the arguments were agreeable because they helped them discover each other's quirks. And to underscore that intimate knowledge, they gave each other nicknames. Conversations were endless, and yet, they were always hungry for more. And all this ensured that Alice felt he had really come into his own.

It was a time of impending transitions. Nitin left soon and gave glowing reports of Bangalore, so Iyengar was planning to join him there. Bakchod got a better job in Gurgaon and had to move out of the city soon. At the home front, Alice's father was mulling retirement and his mother was planning pilgrimages around the country. For all his teenage rebellion, things were unfolding in the prescribed Hindu way. They were all moving to the next step in the ashrama path.

That night, Bakchod slept at Nitin and Iyengar's, leaving their room to Snigdha and Alice. The two of them lay under the blankets, savouring each other's warmth talking about the past, the present and their future. They played their favourite songs on Bakchod's laptop throughout the night.

Alice remembered holding her face in his hands often. Or just running his hands over her body. His hands were itching to feel what his eyes had been pining for, for weeks. When they locked fingers, Alice was surprised that the webbing between his fingers could feel tingly too. Every part of his body seemed to have heightened its sensitivity.

When he ran his fingers through her cascading hair, Alice saw the millions of potential paths that lay ahead of them and every one of them seemed exciting. Elusive adulthood was finally within grasp, Alice felt certain. And he intended to savour every moment of it.

BOOK II

Summer

Seven Years Later

6

Despite sleeping directly under the fan and in only his boxers, little pools of sweat had formed under his chin and armpits, and in the one major fold of his stomach that doubled into his navel. He tried to ignore any sensation caused by the perspiration that was gathering in various parts of his person and will himself to sleep some more, but in vain. So, from the foetal position, he stretched out on to his back, kicked his legs out and put his arms out in search of the dupatta he had covered himself with the previous night. He didn't want to open his eyes but even his arms outstretched to the utmost were unable to find the cloth. He prised his eyes open with great difficulty to find the blurred form of Chikki sitting in the far corner of the double bed.

'Shit ... what is the... what are these... What are you doing here?' garbled Alice, making his search for any cloth more frantic.

'I was sleeping here,' trilled Chikki, handing Alice the dupatta.

'Did I not wake up when you came in?' Alice wiped his body thoroughly twice over.

'I was here already. How did you not notice I was here?' Chikki laughed. Her apartment was quite far away from the centre of the city, so she crashed on Alice's bed if it was too late, inconvenient or expensive to go back home.

'I was too stoned to tell, I guess,' mused Alice. 'So you were here when I tripped over trying to take off my clothes and farted quite audibly?'

'Thank god I slept through that,' guffawed Chikki, making a face. 'I don't think you even switched the light on once.'

'Yep. Hence the tripping and farting.' He wrapped up his upper body up with the dupatta because he still couldn't find any clothes. 'Ei, Chikki, please just go to the living room or something, no… I can't find my clothes.'

'No chance! This whole … you! Wrapped up in that dupatta with those chicken legs and noodle arms. It's really working for me.'

'Shut up. You are looking at a naturally athletic body. Not a steroid-pumped gym bod.'

'I will say that you are in pretty decent shape … considering your lifestyle,' laughed Chikki, rising from the bed. 'There are some people who just naturally pull off excessive body hair. You are definitely one of them.'

'Maybe you could send me a text next time that you are coming over.'

'I did send you a text. You never check your messages,' smirked Chikki.

'Okay, just go and make some tea.'

'What the fuck? I am a guest here. You make tea.'

'If you make chai, I'll make bread-omelette. With cheese.' Alice negotiated.

That was enough to convince her. She skipped away towards the kitchen.

Alice walked into the bathroom to wash his face with cold water. He gargled, rinsed his mouth, and without wiping his face, walked up to the toilet and sat down. As he watched drops of water drip on to his thigh and make their way down the insides of his thighs, Alice wondered if this was adulthood, the feeling of disintegration. The knowledge that the growth phase of one's life is truly over and now is the not-so-slow descent. For a few years now, the high point of his day was the morning dump. The rest of the day was just his mind and his body letting him down in various ways. He wasn't hormonal anymore and so, gradually, he had even stopped making an effort to get laid. He was a stringer for a few news publications. So, he liked his work, but it was rarely the best part of his day.

But how could he qualify as an adult? He had a lot of jobs, but really no career to speak of. He knew now that being just a writer was never a thing, even in nineteenth-century Britain. He wasn't building a career as a journalist, or in advertising or in public relations or even in corporate communication, that safe haven for jaded journalists. He was making ends meet, but as Nitin always reminded him: if he wasn't saving, he wasn't earning. He was still living with his college friends. He had been 'working on his novel' for more than six years now. At thirty, he looked twenty-five, lived like he was seventeen and felt fifty-eight.

He had a spacious toilet. He was grateful for that. And a roommate who took care of most bills and errands. He was extremely grateful for that but tried not to show it. Nitin was tired of taking care of Alice but would probably only give up for good once he had his own child. He was, by nature, very paternal, so he needed to direct that energy towards someone, Alice told himself. Therefore, despite grumbling, and reprimanding and threatening Alice quite often, he still, more or less, managed the logistics of Alice's life.

Today's dump was more than satisfactory, Alice's brain sighed contentedly. After washing his bum with a health faucet, Alice decided to spray himself with water to feel more human again. Having thus bathed on the pot, he realized he had no towel and so he paced around in the toilet, singing film songs, until the water was no longer dripping so he could use his old clothes to wipe himself dry. He had a shelf to himself in the room but he was living out of the travel bag he had packed for his last visit home. He lived a kind of life where, if he didn't dwell too much on its incongruity and lack of direction, it all seemed pretty satisfactory. Not to anyone else but at least to himself.

Nitin was at the breakfast table eating his oatmeal and drinking his glass of orange juice by the time Alice was done cooking breakfast. Chikki brought out a half-empty bottle of ketchup and got to work on the bread-omelette. Alice decided to check his mail before eating because he was still feeling slightly heavy from his munchies late last night. 'Shit, shit, shit,' he groaned. 'I need to come up with some excuse for why I didn't send the book review to Radhika. She seems to have mailed me twice yesterday. How did I miss this?'

'You didn't miss it,' scoffed Nitin. 'You just never check your mails.'

'You could tell her you fell ill,' Chikki said between mouthfuls of banana pancake.

'That's what I always say. If I am falling ill this often, she'll suspect I have AIDS.'

'Hmm… Hey, maybe you could tell her you need more time to reflect on the book because it's so layered and…'

'I already told her it's lame.'

'Can't it be layered and complex in a lame way?'

'No, the lack of layers or complexity is what makes it lame…' explained Alice and then paused. 'Oh … wow … I think I just found my opening line for the review… What's another word for lame?'

'Lame is good, just go with lame. It shows that you are in touch with the youth.'

'Excellent point.' Alice pulled his phone out of his pocket with some difficulty.

'What would you do without me?' sighed Chikki.

Alice clicked reply in response to Radhika's email and decided to write out the review on his phone, but as soon as he started to type, he got a message from Javed.

> J: Did you finish reading it? What do you think?
>
> A: Sorry man, I just haven't had time to sit down with it.

Javed was well into the seventh year of writing his magnum opus, *The Religion of the Ajivikas*, and had only three quarters of an introduction and four slim chapters pockmarked with innumerable notes and references. Alice was supposed to read the fourth chapter's seventy-third rewrite and give feedback that Javed would then condescendingly reject and embark on the seventy-fourth rewrite. The fourth chapter was especially important because it set up Ajivikism in the context of the world religions of the first millennium BCE. He was attempting to situate Ajivikism in the splintered polities of the Mahajanapada period to show how the material conditions of the period radically shaped the philosophy of the Ajivikas.

> J: You are the main reason I haven't been able to finish this bloody book. Worst friend.

A: You aren't able to finish this book because of research. If you would focus on our cult and not worry about history so much, we would be having this conversation on a private jet or a Rolls Royce.

J: Stop fucking around, man.

A: I am serious. Why can't you write a book called Musings of a Mystical Master, or something that can birthe a spiritual franchise, saving me the trouble of working for a living?

J: Why can't you write it yourself and start the cult? I am not stopping you.

A: If I write the book, then that still counts as me working. Defeats the purpose.

J: Whatever. Give me a date so I can bug you again.

A: OK. I'll finish it over the weekend. Remind me on Monday again. Have you made progress on your aphorisms at least? That shit is marketable.

J: Oh god! Don't remind me of those things.

Javed had, for a while, fancied himself as a serious philosopher and wanted to write a book of aphorisms in the manner of his idol Nietszche. Some were good and others were very cringy but Alice liked them because it gave him a starting point for his grand idea of starting a cult. Javed had reneged on his promise of starting a religion, devoting himself to boring and thankless research that Alice had no interest in.

> A: Listen, Twitter is made for this kind of stuff. I'll just tweet your aphorisms out, just two a day, and you'll have a huge following in just a few months.
>
> J: Listen, I will pay you good money to keep those aphorisms out of any public platform.
>
> A: Money! Now we are talking…

Alice smiled to himself and took a couple more bites of his breakfast. He looked up at Nitin and Chikki. 'If you had the opportunity to blackmail someone and extort money. How much would you ask for?'

Nitin didn't even look up at Alice. 'Weren't you supposed to finish writing that review?'

'Shit! Shit! Shit!'

~

Alice spent most afternoons at Anu's place. Even if she wasn't around, she left her keys behind for him. He found it impossible to work in his own room, which was usually trashed. The afternoon was exceptionally humid. He was sticky with sweat despite sitting directly under the fan. The creaking and whirring of the fan served as the perfect white noise to help him concentrate on his work. The room was also always neatly maintained by the domestic help who was fond of Alice as she believed he was Anu's only honest shot at marriage.

Presently, he checked his phone for any emails and saw that Radhika had replied approving the review pending minor edits. He sighed with relief and collapsed back on to the large bean bag. Anu was a filmmaker and lived two floors below Alice. After a failed attempt at dating more than two years earlier, they were now friends with dull and infrequent benefits. Most of the time, though, they hung out platonically, helping each other out with writing, and discussing movies and politics with other friends—for Anu's house was a hub of sorts for a few aspiring and struggling artists from the cinema and music industries.

Everyone Alice knew in the city was someone he had met either at her house or through her in some way. He met Chikki through Bhaskar's bandmate DB, short for double bass. He had met even Bhaskar through Anu, although it didn't seem that way as Alice and Bhaskar behaved like chaddi-buddies. The theatre artists who supplied Alice with set-design work regularly weren't direct contacts of Anu but they were part of Chikki and DB's polyamorous cluster.

Alice was deeply impressed when Chikki first told him about her polyamorous relationship because he had assumed it was about keeping sex fresh by shuffling.

'Are there polyamorous clusters of people closer to my age?' he had asked Chikki. She was still an undergrad.

'Yeah, I am sure there are,' she had said. 'It's actually a very healthy way of living. It's about letting go and making yourself emotionally available to multiple people and derive support and...'

'Wait a second. So a polyamorous relationship is actually like a relationship?'

'Yeah, obviously.'

'So, it's like a serious relationship but with more people?'

'As the word clearly indicates...'

Alice had been thinking more on the lines of a no-holds-barred Roman orgy and was suitably disappointed and, consequently, gave up on the idea. He found the idea of being emotionally available to even one person pretty painful.

Presently, Anu was in the house, and it was populated by Bhaskar, his bandmates DB, his composer-mixer-DJ, and Lanky, the band's saxophonist and resident asshole. Bhaskar slumbered on the divan, resting his head on a bolster next to him, while DB cozied up to Chikki, and Lanky tried to lazily flirt with Anu not with an intent to hit on her but just because he was a natural creep who spoke to all women with a certain lilting drawl.

Most of Alice's days passed in this manner. Unlike many writers, Alice liked to work in the bustle of company. Loneliness was only for reflection and misery. He felt that observing people while writing ignited several triggers for potentially good sentences, no matter what he might have been writing. Sometimes, when his monetary supplies were not completely extinguished and he was thus not motivated to write, he'd pull out one of his half-painted canvasses and stare at it for hours after applying a handful of brushstrokes on it. If he was left alone in the house, more often than not, he would masturbate, smoke pot in her loo, and then spend the rest of the time trying to clear the smell before Anu returned.

The conversation that day was particularly dull because Lanky was holding forth on Elon Musk and the hyperloop. Completely in character, he worshipped corporate bigwigs and maintained that capitalism would make everyone rich. While Alice did agree that travelling underground sounded much safer than being projectiled through the air in a metal container, to say that he felt uncomfortable about corporate altruists was an understatement. He leaned back in the bean bag and closed his eyes, attempting to drift off for a little while. He often fantasized about giving long lectures filled with obscure and pointless philosophy that would be lapped up by Mylapore elites, helping him set up a corporate empire in Javed's name.

Seated on a platform surrounding an ancient peepul tree, Alice surveyed the crowd in front of him. People had come from far and near, princes and paupers, the wedded and the widows. King Prasenjit of Rajagriha and Prince Ajatashatru of Magadha, the joint organizers of the assembly, took their places at the front of the crowd. Alice looked to his right at the white lady with short hair, who nodded at him with a smile and motioned to him to start. Alice flared his nostrils, took a deep breath and cleared his throat. Silence fell.

'You can still your mind when you make your body still.' When Alice spoke, his voice had a little American twang from giving innumerable *pravachanas* at the Pittsburgh Balaji temple. 'By locking your body in eight ways you can unlock the mysteries of your mind.' King Prasenjit's ears perked up. He stood up, folded his hands and said, 'Please teach us your ways, holy master!'

The white lady next to Alice cleared her throat and announced, 'The assembly must realize that it is not so easy to still the body or the mind. All of you must first start off by buying our T-shirts, pyjamas and interior home decorations at fifteen times the price that you would pay in the marketplace at Sravasthi or Rajagriha.' She struck a gong which rang with a soft ping.

Alice opened his eyes. Lanky was done talking and was now forcing Anu, Chikki and DB to watch some mildly offensive content on YouTube. Despite them cringing and trying to push his phone away, he kept shoving it right back into their faces insisting it would get better. Alice tried to look for his phone. It would be a good idea, his brain pointed out, for you to check your upcoming deadlines and be on top of things for once. Alice's search for his phone was beginning to get frantic when Bhaskar pulled the phone out from under his ass and handed it to Alice.

'What's your lazy ass up to today, bro?' asked Bhaskar.

'Just finished writing the review,' yawned Alice.

'Whoa. So staring at the screen long enough for the review to write itself works? I thought it would never be done. Hasn't it been a week since the deadline?'

'Yeah, thankfully Chikki supplied me with the first line.'

'Ah. Show me ... hmm... I like that you say "lame". I, too, thought it was lame.'

Bhaskar had also read the book and was bothered by how insipid it was. It wasn't even worthy of a strong enough feeling like hate, he had said. He read through Alice's review, agreeing occasionally by chuckling or making clucking noises. Alice closed his eyes again.

'What are you thinking about?' asked Bhaskar after a while, nudging Alice in the ribs with his elbow. It was Bhaskar's most annoying habit.

Alice opened his eyes a little and made a face. 'I don't think I've ever told you this but since college I have always dreamed of starting a cult. Javed was supposed to float away to the Himalayas to write esoteric rubbish that I would market and sell to superstitious businessmen. Instead, he abandoned the idea for some stupid historic research, and I am having to suffer the poverty and obscurity.'

'Starting a cult is certainly not the worst idea you ever had.' Bhaskar was encouraging when he wanted to be.

'There are so many thought processes I can appropriate,' mused Alice. 'So many writings I can interpret simplistically to manipulate people.'

'That's good. Put reading those pointless history and philosophy books to some good use. Maybe you don't need Javed. I can see you pulling this off by yourself.'

'Hmmm ... thanks. I'd make a good godman, wouldn't I? Try to imagine me with a longer beard, an

Americanized rural Indian accent and foreigners sitting too close to me and smiling stupidly.'

'A harem of white women could be a good look for you, I don't know… But you seem more like the kind of creepy guy who would arrange orgies and then watch them from the circuit television room wearing a bathrobe and socks.'

'Hahaha … you know, in a way, that sounds really appealing. Actually, having sex with several people must be exhausting. They make it look easy on Porn Hub but I can tell it's a lot of work.'

'Exactly! And even those twenty minutes are after considerable editing. It's not your cup of tea. Leave it to the professionals.'

'That's really sound advice,' agreed Alice. 'So you think I can do this? Will you be my apostle then? My first convert?'

'What's in it for me, though?' asked Bhaskar, putting his deal face on.

'I don't know … Do you have any good ideas? What do you bring to the table?'

'Who's going to infuse your plagiarized bhajans with echo and auto-tune? That's an essential part of every spiritual franchise.'

'Wow, you have completely proved your worth with that amazing idea. I'll offer you thirty per cent stake.'

'Fuck your thirty per cent. Just make me the treasurer of your trust, machaan. I'll make sure there's enough money for orgies and the best VR equipment. Don't ask about the rest.'

Alice had come to gradually move away from looking at life through a lens of good living or poor living and more through the lens of elegant or inelegant coping (elegance and inelegance relative to but not limited by social standards of normalcy).

He often thought about the various coping strategies people around him adopted, so that he might improve upon his own. Anu, he felt, coped by keeping life at arm's length. She was outwardly unemotional, stuck to things she knew well and resisted taking chances of any kind. Chikki, like Bakchod, had the ability to drag life by its collar and take it out partying even when life was tiresome and hungover. And also, if they didn't notice their maladjustment, it probably didn't count. But Bhaskar was a sufferer in that tragic poetic sense. He was very sensitive to every aspect of life and each new conundrum ate away at the already meagre joy he felt. His coping mechanism, though, involved rocking a guitar on stage, so Alice felt there was no sympathy due. Coping mechanisms, like making good music, were a good deal by any standards.

Javed was like Batman. He coped by being rich. For a while, Javed seemed like the person who would manage to get through life with the help of his wits. But when his wits failed him, he would still have money. Javed saw it too. It made its way in one of his earlier aphorisms.

If money can't buy you peace of mind, you're not spending it right.

'I think that works for me. We have a deal.' Alice shook Bhaskar's hand.

'Excellent. Shall we discuss the details over a J?' suggested Bhaskar.

'You ask Anu. She won't let me smoke here.' Alice made a sad face.

'That's because you are clumsy, bro. And you roll fat stinkers. I'll ask her, wait.' He turned to Anu. 'Anu? J?'

'No.'

'Please?'

'Not here. No chance.'

Alice laughed heartily as Bhaskar swore at her under his breath. 'Fine. I guess I'll smoke it by myself when I am home.'

'What the fuck, asshole!' cried Alice indignantly. 'Don't leave me hanging.'

'What am I supposed to do?'

'Let's smoke on the road.'

'No way.'

'Bro.'

'No chance.'

'Bro.'

'No.'

'For friendship?' Alice was crestfallen.

'Fuck off, dude. Not happening.'

~

This was not the first time Alice and Bhaskar were caught smoking pot on the road. However, the previous time, the cop had not been able to identify the smell of pot and they had managed to flick the joint so far away that it wasn't retrievable as evidence. This time Bhaskar mistimed the flick and the joint tamely rolled over right next to the constable's boot. The sub-inspector picked it up and sniffed at it. He smiled beatifically at the two of them and began to coax and caress the joint while ogling at it in the manner of a detective. After fiddling with the joint and fingering it for some more time, he handed it to the constable. The constable flung it to the ground angrily, stubbed it out violently and walked towards Bhaskar to search him. So, Alice walked up to the constable and handed over the rest of the pot as a show of good faith. He took his wallet out, opened it up to make his identity card visible and handed it to the sub-inspector. 'Get into the van,' the sub-inspector said, smilingly.

It was a red SUV with nicely done-up interiors and beige, black and red seats. The dashboard was adorned with a clown bobble-head and a plastic Indian flag with a glittering chakra. The constable got into the driver's seat and the sub-inspector got into the front from the other side. Alice opened the back door and let Bhaskar in before climbing in himself and closing the door. The back windows were not automatic and were half open. 'Right,' called the sub-inspector and they were off.

The ride was rather pleasant as Alice had managed to catch a great buzz by the time they had got caught. The cops didn't say anything and Bhaskar was glaring at him every time Alice caught his eye, so Alice looked out of the window as a strong wind swept his thinning hair back and blow-dried his grizzly beard. The driver drove around the entire colony, even through improbably narrow lanes, in an expert manner. They passed the park that Anu and he had attempted to jog in for barely two weeks more than a year ago. Every time they slowed down or stopped at a signal, Alice tried to scan the traffic for familiar faces. He couldn't do a thorough job as he kept zoning out, his buzz peaking. As they approached the bridge, whose sides were also spots where Alice had smoked, the sub-inspector turned around and said, 'This whole area you saw, that's the area we patrol. The area where you were smoking comes under our beat.'

Alice nodded intelligently and smiled.

'Where did you buy this stuff from?'

'A friend gave it to us.'

'Hmm… Where did he buy it from?'

'Not sure, sir. Somewhere in Anna Nagar, he said.' That was the other corner of the city. They would have no interest in that area.

'Which newspaper do you work for?' He bent his knee and put his leg up on the front seat to turn around and talk to Alice.

'I don't, sir. I freelance for a few papers and magazines.'

'Do you think the papers would be interested in the story of you getting caught?' the sub-inspector smirked. Sitting right beside Alice, the constable laughed uproariously into his ear.

'I'm actually thinking about writing about the experience of riding in a police van,' Alice smiled back. Strangely, the cannabis made him uninhibited. Why can't this happen at parties, his brain grumbled.

'That's a fine idea. Who'll print this?'

'I'll write this for the internet,' said Alice, making a note to pitch it to Radhika.

While they were driving through a parallel main road, the sub-inspector's walkie-talkie screeched to life. It emitted some low-frequency gurgles in a language that could have been Tamil or Klingon. The sub-inspector thumbed a button on the side of his walkie-talkie and barked something equally incomprehensible back. The constable, though, seemed to know where to go. He shifted his weight on to the accelerator and drove with more purpose through the main roads and lanes for some more time, until they spotted a guy standing next to a constable beside the popular hub for working-class commies—Chicago tea stall—and picked them up.

Alice got off and let the constable and the stubbly guy go through to the back seats, and climbed back in. After they drove in silence for a while, the sub-inspector turned around again.

'Domestic abuse case,' he explained in English. 'His wife has been waiting at the station since morning.'

Alice nodded but didn't smile.

'So, what's happening in the news these days?' He took a sip of water from a water bottle and offered it to Alice and Bhaskar, both of whom knew they were supposed to politely decline.

'The news, sir…' said Alice, smiling. 'What's in the news that you wouldn't know about.'

The sub-inspector let out a 'tch' in annoyance. 'We know nothing, boss. The job is so demanding, it's difficult to keep track of the news. There's so much happening these days.'

'Umm … have you been reading about the ISIS, sir?' For some reason that was the only thing that had come to Alice's mind.

'Yeah. That's old news, boss.'

Bhaskar suddenly spoke. 'Sir, actually in Europe, people are converting to Islam so that they can join ISIS.'

This piece of information seemed to be new. 'Are you serious?'

'It's true, sir,' Alice seconded him, even though he didn't really know. 'I think it came on Al Jazeera.'

'But why would they want to do that? Are they being brainwashed?' The sub-inspector was agitated. This seemed to upset the hitherto silent constable.

'Apparently it's the dead-end sedentary lifestyle that these kids lead,' Alice offered. 'Seems to them that these militant organizations offer them a zest for life that's sorely missing.'

'Sons of whores!' he thundered. 'These kinds of things happen in places like Europe and all because they lack a good historic culture and tradition. Of course these things will happen in India also because we have adopted their systems.'

The sub-inspector's scowl soon eased, though, and he stroked his moustache thoughtfully. 'That's very true. It's the Macaulay system of education that's ruining us,' offered the constable in the back seat.

Alice and Bhaskar nodded brightly.

After a good half an hour more of patrolling, they pulled up at the police station. The constable led the domestic abuser into the police station while Bhaskar, Alice and the sub-inspector remained seated in the van.

'See, I don't want to charge you because, well, you know why ... it'll fuck your life up and all that. So, I'll let you go with a piece of advice. Why do you want to smoke near these rich people's houses? They call and complain and do shit like that. Go smoke behind the local station or in a deserted part of the beach. These entitled bastards call the station for every little thing.'

'Noted, sir,' Bhaskar nodded grimly. 'We are really sorry your work was disturbed because of us.'

'Bah, that's all right. This is my job. What about you? Why don't you just smoke cigarettes? This is illegal, right? Why take the risk?'

'That's very true, sir,' Alice nodded vigorously. 'We'll stick to cigarettes from now on.'

'I mean, if you must.' The sub-inspector frowned and appeared a little unsettled. There were low but shrill noises emerging from inside the station. 'But why even smoke, for that matter? Just quit this sort of stuff.'

'That's so true, sir.'

'We'll really try our best, sir.'

The sub-inspector looked rather unconvinced but decided he had had enough. The noises were getting louder and there seemed to be a commotion about. He dismissed the boys and smartly marched back into the police station.

7

Throughout the summer, the outdoors were only tolerable around midnight. The air was still warm and heavy, but the pollution settled and the temperature was on the wane. The roads were practically empty, save for stray dogs, and the cleaners, who were on their way to work. The roads were fairly clean too. Walking under the canopied roads padded with dry leaves, breathing pure air while eyeballing the dogs on the street, and deferentially sidestepping homeless men slumbering in the open, some of them passed out after a bottle of brandy or a hit of smack, was one of Alice's enduring pleasures. And so, he didn't mind the one-kilometre walk to their destination—the venue of Bhaskar's midnight recording concert.

There would be a few patrol vehicles around, too, but the cops were familiar. So that was never much of a problem. Alice always had trouble with Google Maps, so Bhaskar turned the voice navigation on, and they let the confident female voice lead them from Alice's apartment to the venue where the concert was going to be held.

A bearded music producer whom Chikki had met at some shady pub owned a recording studio. Perhaps hoping to score with Chikki or one of her friends, he had suggested holding a small private gig for Bhaskar's band which he would record live for them. They had also invited a few rich friends who could crowdfund the production. Chikki and friends were very impressed. Bhaskar was very nervous. He had been practising the set day in and day out for the whole of last month. Getting the recording right during the concert would save them a lot of money. Anu was helping him make a concert video. This was his one opportunity to get a lot of content out with little investment.

The navigation lady announced the destination about two streets away from the beach. It was an old housing-board quarters building. They made their way through an expansive old lobby and walked three storeys up to the topmost floor. The studio was a large-ish loft padded with foam for soundproofing. A faux-hardwood flooring and false ceiling added to the ambience apart from helping with the sound. The music producer and another guy, presumably a crowd filler, were sitting on the chaise lounge in the far corner talking to DB and Lanky who were seated on a chair and a bean bag respectively. Obscuring them from view were Anu, Chikki and an assistant, who were helping set Anu's camera equipment to face the small stage that had on it microphone stands and a dusty old drum-kit. A strikingly good-looking guy was sitting in front of a large screen fingering some very fancy-looking equipment: a large board with keys, knobs and some LED-studded switches.

Bhaskar waved to Chikki and Anu before making a beeline for the corner where the music producer was. Even before Alice could say hi, his eye spotted the table where the drinks were laid out. He made himself a whisky and soda, topped it with four ice cubes, and walked back towards Anu and Chikki. As he reached them, the door opened and three of Chikki's friends burst into the room screaming, 'Babe!' A lot of hugging and kissing ensued before they were introduced. Alice didn't catch any of their names. Two of them were dressed in gaudy evening wear while the other one wore pants and a blouse.

Since they were trampling all over the wires, Anu suggested Chikki get them some drinks and they all drifted away towards the area where the drinks were kept. From the corner of his eye, Alice spotted the producer make some excuse and walk up towards the girls.

'Need help with anything?' Alice asked Anu, sipping his whisky.

'No, I am good.' She looked really busy.

Alice walked further away towards the wall adjacent to the door to look at an interesting oil painting. It looked amateurish, but it had vigour. It was the painting of a purplish donkey against a black background. Alice liked the subject. It gave the viewer a lot to think about, he felt. The front legs of the donkey were in the midst of a trot while the back legs were completely stationary. That was weird, but it still added to the strangeness of the whole thing. It was clear a child had painted it but hanging it up was still a gutsy move. When he turned around, he saw to his horror that the pretty sound equipment guy was chatting up Anu.

They seemed to have finished with introductions because he said, 'Should I get you a drink? Are you allowed to drink on the job?'

'I prefer not to, especially when I am handling the camera,' Anu replied, smiling and pushing her short hair back.

'Don't you just have to turn them on and walk away once the cameras are set up?' he grinned. The bastard had a disarming smile.

'That's true. I'll get a drink when the crowd clears.' Anu turned away to fiddle with her camera.

'Allow me,' he said charmingly.

Alice walked over to Bhaskar who was making weird noises to warm his vocal chords.

'Bhaskar! Bhaskar!'

'What, da?' Bhaskar was poring over his set list.

'There's some pretty boy chatting up Anu.'

'Hmm...' Bhaskar wasn't paying attention, so Alice shook him.

'Look. There. There. Anu and Pretty Boy. Pretty Boy and Anu. Talking.'

'Yeah, yeah I see them... Okay... So what?' Bhaskar was fairly even-tempered even when he was stressed.

'What do you mean "so what"?' asked Alice agitatedly. 'What should I do?'

'Come up to me after the third song and give me this glucose water.' Bhaskar was back to poring over his set list.

'Don't be a smartass. What if she goes back home with him tonight?' Alice tried to pack as much panic as he could into his voice.

'Well, then go talk to her. Beat the Pretty Boy.'

'No, I don't want to, you know, like ... cramp her style and all.'

'Cramp her style? Really?' Bhaskar chuckled.

'You know, if that's what she wants, I won't interfere.' He didn't want to be seen making an effort with her. Shame, cried his brain. I hope she does go back with Pretty Boy.

'Good,' said Bhaskar. 'Leave her alone and just maintain eye contact with me onstage so I can signal you for the glucose water...'

'Fuck your glucose water, man.'

'Fuck you, man. Don't fuck around. This is my big night,' said Bhaskar through gritted teeth. 'So you don't even have to be a good friend; just be a decent human being. Okay? Leave Anu alone and help me get my shit together tonight. Now, how many people are going to be around?'

Alice looked suitably chastised. 'Anu wanted about ten people casually lounging around the place while you guys play.'

'Hmm. People are trickling in slowly. I think we should start soon.'

'Calm down. We have all night. Don't be in a hurry.'

'Cool, cool, thanks.'

'Have you gone through the set list?'

'Yeah. Like a hundred times. I am feeling confident about all the songs.'

'Good. And the energy is high?'

'Yep!'

'Good. Then let's talk about Anu and Pretty Boy.'

'I'll seriously punch you, man. Not kidding.'

~

The concert started about half an hour later by which time Alice's anxiety about Anu and Pretty Boy was starting to peak. Thankfully, as soon as Bhaskar, DB and Lanky took their positions, Pretty Boy had to go back to the fancy equipment which was now being manned by the producer. Bhaskar cleared his throat and checked the mic. He was a different person on stage. His general discomfort with existence disappeared completely once he was up there. When he introduced himself and his band, Alice led the hoots and cheers. DB and Lanky made their way to the elevated platform that served as a stage and took their positions on either side of Bhaskar.

Suddenly, Alice noticed that Anu had turned the cameras on and retired to the blind area which was right next to Pretty Boy's station! Alice was stuck at the other end near the chaise lounge sipping at his whisky glass that he couldn't refill because he would have to cut across the cameras to reach the table.

Bhaskar began with one of Alice's favourites but Alice didn't pay much attention through the first song as he was mostly trying to bend his neck to catch a glimpse of what Anu and Pretty Boy were up to. He was, however, careful in a way that would also seem like he was enjoying the music.

Pretty Boy seemed genuinely interested in the music, but maybe he was putting on a good show because Anu was friends with the band. When Bhaskar finished the song, Alice whistled with one hand and put the glucose bottle up for Bhaskar to see, and shook it. Bhaskar wound his free arm at the wrist a few times to say he'd take it after the next song, or maybe the one after that. Alice didn't even wait for the next song to start before getting back to spying.

Anu and Pretty Boy were cheering a lot between songs, but during the song, Pretty Boy took the opportunity to lean really close to her to whisper into her ear. To Alice's dismay, she was whispering back. At the end of the third song, Alice walked up to the stage and handed Bhaskar the bottle of glucose water.

'They are fraternizing a little too much,' whispered Alice.

'What the fuck is wrong with you? Now … how was I?' hissed Bhaskar, drinking the water in large gulps.

'Really good. Keep it going,' Alice answered confidently.

'Yeah? It was good?'

'Yep. Absolutely. Really good escalation. Good energy. The general energy here is really good. So, you know, just keep the energy high.'

Bhaskar looked rather unsure about how much attention Alice had been paying to him onstage, but he had to return the bottle and get back on stage.

Anu and Pretty Boy walked up to the cameras and changed the memory card and the batteries. Everyone took a break and Alice found an opportunity to refill his glass. He took a shot of whisky and filled his glass with another large. His mood improved considerably.

In the warmth of the ascending buzz, Alice felt more human and decided he would try to be a good friend and pay attention to the concert. It was best to give Anu up as a lost cause and enjoy himself even if he couldn't be happy for her. After one super-melodic yet slowish song that tested Alice's resolve and made his neck twitch in Anu's direction owing to the fact that it was their favourite, Bhaskar's next two songs were fast and peppy, and Alice could lose himself in grooving and head-banging. Alice looked at his phone.

A: Just tell me in simple words.

J: The whole idea behind establishing Ajivikas in the midst of the Sramanic tradition is to talk about how problems of wages, labour, debt and money influenced philosophy and religion in axial age world religions. Ideas like karma and redemption were attempts to understand the nature and source of money. Money is how we measure debts and so the very nature of debt became the subject of deep philosophical speculation. But in later ages when the system went back to a rural credit system from an urban market system, the meaning of such concepts acquired more spiritual connotations and the material meanings were lost.

J: But if I explain all this to you before you read it how will I know how the text reads?

J: At least tell me what you thought of the three pages that you read?

A: So far, in these three pages, you've basically established the meanings of the word Ajivika as wage-earning professional and the word Sramana as being derivative of Srama or labour. But I am a little exasperated it took you three pages to establish just this. It's reasonably common knowledge, people will take your word for it. Trust me.

J: There is a lot of nuance that gets left out when you say it like that.

A: These three pages have seventeen citations. Stop swinging your dick in my face, man. Just give me the gist. I can live with it.

J: Fuck you.

And he hadn't said anything after that. Alice often told Javed that the problem with his book was that it was too difficult to read. 'I think even academic works should be easily understandable to everyone,' Alice once told him sagely.

'Understandable to all other academics in the field,' Javed scoffed. 'Everyone doesn't mean every idiot like you.'

Bhaskar breezed through the concert, with DB and Lanky in top form. Alice was sure that although Bhaskar would whine and crib and agonize over it, they would not need patchwork or re-recording. When the concert was over, Bhaskar hugged his bandmates, shook hands and took selfies with a bunch of people while Alice picked the glucose water, drank half of what remained in the bottle and took the rest up to Bhaskar, handing it over to him. Meanwhile, the producer came up to them and whisked them away for a few shots of vodka, after which a ravenous Bhaskar stuffed his face with finger food while Alice forced him to listen to the tale of his amazing resolve in the face of intense temptation. Fortunately for Bhaskar, Anu and Chikki suddenly appeared out of nowhere, with DB and Pretty Boy in tow. Thankfully, Lanky was nowhere to be seen. Alice finished two more drinks, nibbling on tikkas, while the others gushed about their performance. Bhaskar and DB customarily grumbled about how they weren't at their best because of the quality of the equipment or the back-up instrumentalist/vocalist. The gushing then became tempered by a fair bit of bitching that suddenly seemed to make everyone sweaty and, consequently, suddenly aware that the air conditioning had been turned off. In a short while Bhaskar announced that he was tired and needed to head home to crash. He would leave with DB and Chikki, who lived roughly in the same area.

'Anu, what about you?' Bhaskar asked.

'I can drop her home,' Pretty Boy offered.

Alice tried to sip at his already empty glass nonchalantly, pretending to be interested in the purple donkey. The contrast between the dynamism of the front legs and the centralizing poignancy of the back legs began to manifest its appeal to Alice.

'Ummm… Actually, I'm going back with…' Anu jerked her arm nonchalantly in Alice's direction. 'We live in the same building.'

Alice looked up in surprise to see Pretty Boy's face fall before a practised recovery followed by a 'Cool, see you around, then.' Bhaskar, Chikki and DB went along with him, leaving Alice with Anu, who was still sipping on her wine.

'Sorry, I was just trying to make an excuse. Did you have other plans?' asked Anu.

'Plans?' Alice laughed, a little louder than merited because of how relieved he was with Anu's decision. 'Should I call a cab?'

'We can walk back, no?' Anu tied back her hair and picked up her handbag.

'Yeah, I prefer that too.'

~

Anu's flat was a large one-BHK, tastefully furnished with low-lying chairs and a divan. She brought out a bottle of Old Monk. They bottoms upped the first drink and refilled.

'Hey Anu, I am only asking you this because we are really drunk and drinking some more…'

'Asking me what?'

'Asking you a thing I am about ask?'

'Which is what?'

'I'll tell you that if you let me! God! Just let me speak, will you? So … why didn't you go back with Pretty Boy from the party?'

'Pretty Boy! Haha. Is that what you are calling him?'

'Well, he is pretty,' Alice said defensively.

'I wouldn't say pretty… Handsome … dashing, maybe,' teased Anu, aware of how it annoyed Alice.

'Whatever, since he is so handsome and dashing, why didn't you go back with him?'

'Oh god! Do I have to answer that?'

'No … not really. Why look a gift horse in the mouth right?' said Alice, laughing.

Anu became very silent. In the dim yellow light of the living room, she poured another drink and stared deeply into the glass, looking like an NRI woman in a nineties' crossover cinema in her chiffon saree and cropped hair. Alice continued to sip his drink as his brain laughed at him for wrecking his first chance of sex in months. Suddenly, Anu gulped the rest of her drink and turned to Alice.

'Can you sit next to me?'

Alice joined her on the divan, and she curled up by his side and thrust her head into his neck. He adjusted her head slightly for comfort and left his hand there, stroking the hair around her ear softly. She nuzzled his neck softly, inadvertently pressing on a nerve on his shoulder causing him an intense pain that he didn't express, careful not to ruin the moment. He dipped his shoulder slightly and readjusted her head.

'It's so tiring to aspire to things,' Anu whispered. 'My work takes a lot out of me and after that, I am scared to be in a space where I need to have expectations from another person. I am so battle-weary that I don't want another situation where I actually have to try to make something happen with a person I like. Was the sex good? Will he call me? And even if it does work out, where is the relationship going? How do we feature in each other's lives? I am so fucked up that I actually like the stability of our non-relationship. I like that I can sleep with you, or not, without the hope of a relationship. Your choices, habits and life don't affect me at all. And impressively, you are not pushy about sex.'

Alice smiled. 'Hey! I resent the stereotype of the sex-crazy male. We have other needs that trump our sexual needs. Like my need to put my leg over someone when I sleep. It's amazing it doesn't bother you.'

'I am a deep sleeper, I guess. It never really bothered me. I am also willing to put up with some stuff to keep our non-relationship going. You are so lazy and directionless that you don't even make an attempt to date other women. That suits my ego and my own laziness and directionlessness, I guess.'

'There is nobody to date. Anyone close to my age is married or dating someone who's not a hobo. I wish I could be one of those dirty, rotten scoundrels, but I have no charm or etiquette. What I have is an inborn lack of talent honed and shaped by years of accumulating insecurities. I am somewhat of an expert at leaving women deeply unimpressed, even if I say so myself.'

'That, you are … hmm… and I am glad, because I like this.' Anu lay down on the divan pulling Alice down next to her. He drew her close to him, put her head on his chest and hugged her, instinctively putting his right leg over her hip. He looked down at her and saw her looking up at him.

'I think you are beginning to grow fond of me,' Alice teased her.

'I've always been fond of you.' Anu kissed him on the cheek.

'Is that why you came back with me instead of Pretty Boy?' he grinned.

'No, I hang out with you because I am fond of you. I sleep with you because I hate myself.'

Alice laughed, and then made a face. 'Wow, that really hurt.'

'Shut up. You know what I mean.'

'No … no I don't. I am deeply offended.' He drew her closer and hugged her tightly again. She ran her hand over his chest.

'Ummm … I am super-drunk and super-tired…' slurred Alice to underscore his drunkenness. Anu was quite inactive in bed and would just lie still and expect Alice to do all the work.

'Oh thank god,' Anu moaned with relief. 'I am really drunk and sleepy too. Can we cuddle until I fall asleep?' Alice was clumsy and inattentive in bed, but he cuddled like a god.

Two hours later, Alice was still awake, smoking up the remnants of an earlier joint, staring at the fan and occasionally brushing away strands of Anu's hair that snuck up his nose. He was so stoned and drunk and sleepy that he couldn't sleep at all. Thoughts came to him in avalanches, consuming him to such an extent that it was enough to prevent him from sleeping, but then, it would leave him dry in a few minutes only to attack him just as he was beginning to fall asleep again.

He cozied up to Anu a little more and pondered his reason for coming back home with her. Well, because she is literally the only woman on earth who'll sleep with you, his brain smirked. But they hadn't had sex. Nor did he really want to. And even earlier, during the recording concert, he could have made an attempt to talk to any of the other women instead of obsessing about Pretty Boy and her. Maybe there was truth to what Anu said about not having the energy to hope. That is perhaps why people got married, because adulthood is in a way the loss of the ability to derive excitement from hope, anxiety, rejection and dejection; ultimately, it is the loss of energy to go down a path that seems to lead to a kind of pointless reflectiveness that can only ever feed the ego in a life starved of meaning.

Only this non-relationship could give him the freedom to drift along while still hugging the beaches even if only temporarily and precariously. And drift along he had to because he was no voyager. Like Nitin often said, some people live dangerously, placing all their bets on one passion, a partner, a dream or a subject. Others hedge their happiness, refusing to see destinations and deriving happiness from milestones, increasing the possibilities of happiness by diversifying in their journeys. Nitin was worried Alice was doing neither. Which was true. Since with meandering, there are no milestones, only signposts. And so, Alice's happiness always seemed to come from moments that could be told as great stories.

While Javed had still been planning to write his comparative religious philosophy book on the Ajivikas, he decided to go on a road trip with Alice, one that would connect the six great Indian cities of the mid-first millennium BCE. He wanted to write it as a travelogue, inspired by some obscure American rock 'n' roll novel. They drove from Sravasti to Rajgir before giving up. Their car had broken down at night in the middle of a wooded area and there was no village in sight. Although absolutely nothing eventful happened, it was fun coming up with different stories about what could have happened, and that was when Alice decided that he should live life in a way that he could accumulate the most number of stories. Like all other affirmations in his life, he never actually managed to follow through. Still, by hook or by crook, over the years he managed to scrape together a good handful of cherished signposts in his life.

Like when he was lathi-charged at a protest. When the policeman turned his attention to another protestor, Alice could have run away to the safety of the smaller roads, but he saw the lathi slip out of the policeman's hand. In a split second, Alice, still smarting and teary from the whacks on his back and calf, made the decision to beat the policeman really hard on his back with a double-handed swing and then threw the lathi lengthwise, knocking him off his feet, giving himself enough time to disappear into the crowd. He kept running for two kilometres until he couldn't run anymore, puked under a tree, and crawled up to a sympathetic auto guy who took Alice home. He then had to shave his head and face and skip town for three weeks until he was sure no one was looking for him and ever since, has only sported a full beard and never a goatee or long hair.

Seeing the Maheshwar fort light up on Diwali night from a boat on the Narmada river with Snigdha—that was another great memory. They had stayed in a lodge that had rooms for seventy-five rupees a night, staying awake through the night, not drinking or making out for the fear of someone breaking into the room and murdering them, or recording them to sell as porn later, prompting Snigdha to commit suicide and Alice to turn into a vigilante who would have to bust trafficking rings in Eastern Europe.

Alice liked to live a life that could accommodate both the chaos and the placidity in his being. He needed both. His non-relationship accommodated most of his needs. He got solitude in misery and company in joy. Ignoring the bad sex and occasional frights of skewing status quo, it was a great place to be in. He also harboured hopes of perhaps writing a screenplay one day and getting Anu to direct it. They both lamented the fact that there were no longer any mythological films being made in the country. Maybe they could fix that. Now that *Baahubali* had been made, they could at least dream.

Sometimes, just for kicks, he wondered what would happen if he did manage to build a successful cult around Javed. A small group of fairly wealthy followers was not that hard to assemble if one knew how to go about it. He had read the *Apprenticed to a Himalayan Master: A Yogi's Autobiography*, and several other books apart from reading in detail over the internet how Osho and others exploited the legal loopholes of foreign countries to their best advantage. He had studied branding and consumer behaviour in college, which helped him understand corporate empires built by other bearded messiahs. It was just about selling books, clothes and retreats. Both consciously and unconsciously, he had been training for this since college. If he could toss his middle-class apprehensions out of the window and just take a glorious leap of faith, maybe … just maybe he could really do it. Mansions. Circuit television orgies. Persona non grata status. Courtroom drama. More books. Assurance that the one thing he would not die of was boredom. And the best part was that he would always be behind the scenes. Javed had good stage presence, good screen presence. He was just crazy enough to be newsworthy but not so crazy as to attract unwanted attention.

Javed had given up on starting a religion, but Alice felt it was just crazy enough to work. If he could do it by himself, Alice often mused, he would do it. But it was impossible to fake the junoon. The one time Javed had had a bad mushroom trip, Alice was convinced that his friend was on the verge of some kind of enlightenment. He sat quietly for hours facing a corner of the cottage they were staying in. After several hours of furtive glances and eerie silences, Javed had begun to whisper feverishly: 'Niyati, sangati and bhava. The seven-fold matrix. I saw it, man. I saw the web come together and then come apart again.'

Alice tried to get Javed to drink some glucose water. 'I can barely hear you, Javed,' he said. 'Why don't you drink some of this and then we can talk?'

Javed took the glass from Alice's hand and took a very small sip. Then, he said, 'Silence and the abyss. The mother and the father. I saw them. They spoke to me in metre. And the metres formed a matrix.'

While he slowly finished the glass, he said many more things, but presently, Alice couldn't remember any of it. But he was sure that what he did remember was enough to get started. There were also all those aphorisms Javed wrote. The metres that formed his matrix. The bad trip had led to a good few months of creativity—it just flowed. The aphorisms were vague and obscure; they all made just enough sense to start a cult, but it was still nonsensical enough to keep the cult going. At the centre of the whole matrix was Alice the Rock. The rock that could build a church or churn an ocean. Alice 2.0. If adulthood would not come to him the prescribed way, he would seize it in the manner of great ascetics. But within months, tragedy struck twice. Snigdha left to study abroad; then Javed read a book that completely changed his views about spirituality and religion. Alice had been drunk, stoned and pining over his lost chance at suggesting a long-distance relationship with Snigdha when Javed announced that he was no longer interested in starting an ascetic religion because he could see through the sociology of spirituality.

'See I was always impressed with the Axial Age. Well I know that's a problematic term, but just as a reference point for, you know, the first millennium BCE, the period where all of the major world religions were birthed. I thought that the period was amazing because of widespread urbanization and the democratization of philosophy. But think about it. The popularity of philosophy is not the sign of a golden age but the sign of an age marred by intense ethical confusions about life and existence itself. The shunning of material pursuits to eye something that went beyond mere ephemerals is itself a sign of rampant and all-pervasive materialism that demands the commodification of spirituality in order to make itself a worthy opponent to said materialism. If such rampant ethical and moral confusion didn't exist, there would be no one commissioning and popularizing such intense works of spiritual pursuit. The period that I assumed was the pinnacle of human thinking was actually the one most marred by meaningless wars and invention of coinage that would change human relationships forever by valuing porous morality against precious metal.' All of that went completely over Alice's head. 'What I mean is that I am no longer interested in starting some major religion. What I want to do is write a history of the Ajivika religion that is not really about the Ajivikas at all. Instead, it will be a scathing critique of the society and social conditions that have birthed modern religions.' He pulled out his red book and stroked its spine. '"Instead of ordering the rich to put limits on acquiring material goods, spirituality focuses on lecturing the poor that those material possessions were never essential to begin with. No wonder these kings and merchants loved ascetics so much. Kings and merchants were in the occupation of leaving people with nothing and these ascetics came along and told people that's exactly how it should be anyway.

"And once you see that these ascetics coming up with such zany ideas were kings to begin with, then you really start to see the scam."'

~

By the time Alice went back in the morning, Padma had already reached home from the airport and was eating breakfast with Nitin. They had retired her nickname on being told by some activist-y friends that it was more problematic than funny. On seeing him, Padma ran up to Alice and punched him really hard in the shoulder.

'You trashed my house, asshole!'

'Owww … that fucking … owww … okay, okay, I'll clean up. Sorry, I didn't know you'd be home already. How was your trip?'

He hugged her and walked into the kitchen to fix himself some breakfast.

'Hey Alice!' Padma called after him. 'Guess who I met in Milan…!'

Alice stopped in his tracks and traced his steps back out of the kitchen.

'Who…?'

'I can tell from your face that you've already guessed and that, too, correctly.' Padma was smirking; Nitin was grinning too.

'Isn't she in the US?'

'Stopping over at Milan on her way to India to do a project here in the Pallikaranai marshes.'

'What? Here?' Alice asked, pointing in the general direction of the marshlands.

'Yep.'

'Recently broken up. Asked a lot about you.'

'No!'

'What, I thought you'd piss your pants with excitement.' Nitin was surprised at Alice's reaction since he had missed Alice's mental monologue a few hours earlier at Anu's place.

'No!' Alice cupped his face and pretended to sob. 'I was all ready to sever all connections with my past and become the enlightened Alice 2.0.'

'Shut up! And do something to your face and hair. She'll be here in two weeks. This might just be your last chance to find someone and settle down.'

'What part of me looks like I am ready to settle down?'

'Your soul is screaming for help.' Padma laughed.

'Bakchod is going to become intolerable if he finds out about this. He has been predicting a *Before Sunset*-like serendipitous rekindling of our flame for a long time now. He's going to feel vindicated.' Alice cringed while shaking his head.

'I know! He is the first person I messaged after I met Snigdha. He was cackling like a witch.' Bakchod was still in Delhi, or one of Delhi's satellite cities to be precise, married and running his own entrepreneurial venture with his father-in-law's capital. He still retained the propensity to bug Alice by sending several minute-long voice messages if Alice didn't reply to his texts in less than five minutes. Despite having his own married life to take care of, he was still annoyingly invested in Alice's personal life. The fact that he was almost thirty and still single ensured that every friend, acquaintance and their dog felt it was okay to advise Alice or even set him up unasked because it was considered a favour.

'Did you get me a hip-flask?' asked Alice, trying to change the subject.

'Yes. But can I please tell you one last time that nobody drinks wine out of a hip-flask?'

'I do.'

'No. But, you don't.'

'I mean, I will have done. So the future-me is saying I do.'

'But if the present-me has reasoned with you and prevented the future-you from making a futuristic ass of yourself, then the future-you cannot, in fact, say I do.'

'Wow. I forgot you were good at this. I was having such a good time without you. I can't believe Nitin let you back into our lives.' He turned to Nitin. 'You sold me out for sex, man. Some BFF.'

'Legitimate sex. Almost two years' worth of legitimate sex.' Nitin smiled as he said this, and then winked at Padma.

'Okay, I appreciate the hint but don't worry, I haven't forgotten our anniversary. I already got you something,' Padma said in a reassuring tone.

'Oh, great! Show me.'

'No. Obviously not until the day after. But you can see all the stuff I bought for myself meanwhile.' Padma picked her suitcase up and pulled Nitin by his hand all the way down the corridor to their room.

8

After more than an hour of intense internal deliberations, Alice decided he would shave. He turned on the light atop the mirror cabinet and lathered his face once only to change his mind and wash it off. But after changing his shirt thrice he decided he would wear not only the first shirt but also shave. And trim the hair around his ears. Or not. The prospect of meeting Snigdha after many years made him even more nervous and unsure of himself than he typically was. He lathered his face again because the repetitive massaging of his cheeks with his badger-hair shaving brush made his world feel a little smaller.

You really shouldn't be messing around so close to dinner, his brain warned and continued, but I am also deeply unhappy with this look. So, he lathered his face again and washed it off again, the front of his T-shirt now drenched with his indecision. His brain reached a compromise with itself: just take those scissors and trim the cheek beard. You look like an overgrown foetus for at least three days when you shave, but right now your beard's making your cheeks look puffy. He looked at both his cheeks alternately in the mirror and, with a silent prayer, put his scissors to work. Predictably, in an effort to maintain symmetry, he cut off way more than he intended to. And so, he was forced to deliberate a complete shave yet again.

After days of careful contemplation, he had finally told Anu that Snigdha was in town and that he was planning to meet her. But he told her when Bhaskar was around, so she, perhaps, had no choice but to pretend to be okay with it and even wish Alice luck. He wanted to send her a longish explanatory text, but that would be really weird, he decided, as they never texted, living in such proximity as they did. He hoped to talk to her the previous night, but she had been called away for a meeting and passed out too early on account of too much nervous smoking. But it had been close to a year since they had even had sex, and barely two months ago she had gone on a dinner date with someone her parents were hoping she'd consider marrying. So, Alice felt it was only fair he did what he wanted to as well. But the more forcefully he told himself this, the less sure he felt.

Back to being unable to decide whether or not to shave even after a further half an hour of auto debate, he walked out to the living room where Nitin and Padma were watching a poorly made web series based on an indulgently written book that had recently become a rage across the country. Both of them loved the show and never failed to chuckle appreciatively at the inane dialogues.

After several attempts by Alice to catch their attention, Nitin paused the show and they both turned around to scowl disapprovingly at Alice.

'Oh, god! It's so patchy,' tutted Padma.

'When will you buy a new trimmer?' asked Nitin irritably.

'Should I just shave?'

'No!' cried the two of them in unison. Alice left them to their show and went back into his room.

Alice returned to his room and checked his phone. He still had an hour before he needed to leave for the bar where he was to have his dinner with Snigdha. She was going to come over for lunch to their house over the weekend but was enthusiastic about meeting Alice for dinner a few days earlier. He was worried he would end up shaving if he didn't occupy himself with something, so he decided to call Bakchod and let him ramble for a good half an hour. The phone rang twice before Bakchod picked up. 'Did you call for a pep talk?'

Alice smiled to himself and said, 'Something like that. What's been up with you?' There was a lot of noise on Bakchod's end of the line. 'Listen, I am in a meeting. No time for small talk or pep talk. I know you'll do great. Just don't be like how you are and you'll be fine. Try to remember what you were like seven years ago. Cheers. Bye.' Bakchod hung up and Alice sighed. He was expecting it to be much easier than this. Now he had no choice but to try and talk to Javed. It wasn't the best idea, but it would probably be worth it just to hear Javed make desperate attempts to take an interest in Alice's life.

'Hi, Javed. What's been up?' Alice called before he could contemplate shaving once again.

'Oh, so you finally read my chapter?' Javed's voice boomed from the other end. He sounded pleased. Alice smacked his forehead.

'Ummm … yeah. Yes, I did. Finally…' Alice struggled to think of something to say.

'And … what did you think?' asked Javed impatiently. Alice smacked his forehead again. He should have just watched some porn to kill time instead of calling Javed.

'It's a definite improvement from the previous version, that's for sure.' Alice tried to sound confident. 'Well, you know, a few typos here and there, but you don't have to worry about that now. It's all coming together pretty well.'

'Even the concluding paragraph?' Javed asked.

Alice gritted his teeth and took a deep breath. 'About that! That final paragraph did make me think, you know … It did make me wonder if it could be a little shorter—'

'Really?' Javed exclaimed. 'You want it even shorter?'

'Well, you know, not exactly shorter per se … but … it could even be longer, you know… But either way, you certainly need to shine light on the crux of what you discuss. How you do it is really up to you. I don't want to get too controlling with my advice you know…'

'Ah, okay. That makes sense, I guess. Tell me this, what, according to you, was the crux of the chapter?'

'Wow! Just one? That's... It's difficult to... Maybe we could discuss a bunch of salient issues but ... hey! One sec ... I think Padma's calling me about the dirty dishes in the sink. Sorry, I got to go. But I'll call back and talk this through with you. I have a lot of things to say.' He hurriedly cut the call. Then he decided to be true to his made-up story and wash the dirty dishes before Padma lost her shit. He put on some old Hindi songs to make the task more bearable: Raj Kumar delineated the virtues of alcoholism to Meena Kumari. It was one of his father's favourite songs that never failed to scandalize his mother. The suggestions on his playlist to follow the song were also great, and he managed to wash, rinse and dry all the dishes before checking the time, only to realize that it would be best to call an auto now since he didn't have enough time to take a bus.

He walked out into the utility area balcony and called out, 'Is anyone free? Drop-off at TNagar!'

On the other side of the road, the lights of one autorickshaw turned on and the engine revved to life. On his way out, Alice took a long, hard look at himself in the mirror, also hoping Snigdha's standards had dropped considerably or that her rebound eye would make him look passable.

~

Throughout the auto ride, Alice shook his right leg compulsively. Obsessing continuously about what he was wearing, he realized in a short while that he wasn't wearing his new underwear that he had bought for today and instead had on the one he had been wearing since morning; he hadn't even powdered or cologned his balls, presumptuous as it may have been. His phone vibrated in his pocket. A message from his father on the family WhatsApp group enquiring about his day followed by a photograph of the beach during their evening walk from his mother. Alice sent some thumbs ups and heart emojis right away and tried to distract himself by what he could say about his day. But he couldn't stay on that thread of thought for long. He was too nervous about meeting Snigdha.

Maybe they'd finish dinner, and she would just tell him that she was glad they had broken up and should stay that way. Or she would get a call from her ex, and they'd patch up right in front of him like in a bad Hollywood excuse-for-comedy. Perhaps she would tell him that they could see each other only if he could pinky swear that he had gotten better at sex. Would he take a chance, or would he admit that the years had only made him worse? He decided he needed to actively distract himself. He closed his eyes and took deep breaths.

Alice idealized Snigdha's and their time together to an extent where he couldn't have a serious relationship since, but Padma believed it was more than that. 'Maybe it's like a soulmate thing,' she often said. 'Why don't you try and contact her?' Nitin, on the other hand, held dismissively that Snigdha was only one in all of Alice's failed attempts at long-term relationships, but he did concede that

Alice's time with Snigdha was better than any attempt before or since.

Alice himself wasn't sure. The fact that he was constantly thinking of her but was unwilling to contact her was certainly not indicative of healthy emotions. But he didn't think he idealized their time together. It was perfect while it lasted and ended on a high without much strife. It was magical and rare to achieve such a combination, as he would discover in the subsequent half of the decade.

They had a certain rhythm in their relationship that they could fall into very easily. They were hungry for time they could spend in each other's company, so there was no space for jealousy or worry, and disappointments were always cushioned by more quality time spent together. It lasted less than a year, but it felt like a lifetime. She had moved in with Padma when Nitin left for Bangalore. She worked on her applications when Alice left for work and their evenings were spent exploring the city until the winter got really cold and then it was spent entirely in the warmth of their bed with Padma or Bakchod supplying them with hot spicy tea.

And then, when it was time for her to leave, Alice surprised himself by expressing an unwillingness to try and make a long-distance relationship work. Snigdha, too, offered no resistance, and they parted with mutual assurances of keeping in touch via email because Alice was unwilling to join Facebook and Snigdha said nobody was really on Orkut anymore. They did, of course, send each other mails where they tried to make up for suppressed emotion with detailed descriptions and attempts at poesy or humour. Eventually, when they got busy with other relationships, communication withered.

At times, Alice wondered how different his life would be if only he had not expressed a disinclination for a long-distance relationship. That his general happiness in his personal life could be determined so hugely by one instance of complacence always troubled him. But, at other times, when work came easy and the weather was good, he didn't mind so much the way his life was going. He tried to take comfort in the fact that he had a variety in experiences without bogging himself down with the failure of all of them.

'Our regular route will delay us by seven minutes. Should I take the alternate route?' asked the autorickshaw driver.

'Sure,' replied Alice. 'Is there a political rally blocking us?' he added.

'No, office traffic. Peak hour, sir,' he was told.

'Even now?' Alice asked, surprised.

'Peak hour is for three to four hours,' said the driver. He continued, 'Plch … what's happening to our city? Sir … it's not our city anymore. People from other states have devoured it.'

'So true…' mumbled Alice and refrained from chatting any further, unsure if his neophyte Tamil would actually pass scrutiny. When they reached the appointed destination, he was able to identify the bar easily as it was a small road and the bar, too, sported a garish neon sign to attract moth-like humans. Or humans like moths, perhaps.

Alice saw her the moment he entered the premises of the restaurant as she had taken a table right under the stock exchange board. Also, it was a weekday and the bar was almost empty. Snigdha was dressed in a tasteful turquoise top and shapely cotton pants. She was carrying a stole and a handbag, but she wasn't wearing her glasses nor was her hair tied up. He smiled and waved. As he walked up to her, she got off her chair and, grinning broadly through squinted eyes, embraced him. Alice lingered and thought that, for a couple of seconds, she did too, but suddenly, sensing a little movement and assuming she was drawing back, withdrew. In that split second, however, Alice felt Snigdha had only begun to draw back deliberately after he did and, perhaps, she had only slightly twitched involuntarily, but they were already drawing away from each other and he would just have to follow through and try to look for other signs.

'Has it really been seven years…!' exclaimed Snigdha as soon as they sat down.

'Yeah, more I think,' Alice said, smiling at a paper napkin he was fiddling with. 'Even *Boyhood*'s released.'

'But the world was supposed to end before that.' Snigdha smiled brightly.

'I thought the world would definitely end when we won the World Cup.'

'I wanted to call you when we won.'

'You should have,' Alice said, smiling more widely. 'I should have. I wanted to call you too.'

'Hmm…' sighed Snigdha. 'And then the elections here and the elections back there…'

'We've survived some intense times, huh?'

The bartender glided over to their side, took their order and slid back out of view.

'So … what have you been up to?' asked Snigdha, squinting and trying to make herself heard over a garish song playing particularly loudly that had replaced the blues number playing until then.

'Well, drifting along you know. Freelancing is nice. Placid water and gentle winds … I did my Masters…'

'Yeah, I heard. Congrats.'

'No, I meant that as an explanation for why I don't have a job,' quipped Alice.

'Haha. I haven't had a job in the last seven years,' Snigdha added hurriedly.

'Yeah, but being jobless abroad in pursuit of academic dreams is romantic and sexy. When you see white people do things you can't afford, it's okay. But seeing rich brown people do the same is hard to stomach…'

Snigdha laughed and said, 'That does sound bad.'

'I am brown trash.' Alice nodded with mock sadness.

'Oh, I really do hope that phrase catches on. Tell me about your Masters.'

'No. Too boring and not at all of consequence. You tell me. Is grad school exactly like PhD comics?'

'Like you won't believe.' She smiled. Their drinks arrived; they clinked glasses and mumbled cheers awkwardly as their eyes locked for the first time that evening. Snigdha took a sip of her whisky and added a little more soda to it.

'Grad school is exhausting. I'd actually look forward to finishing it off if I didn't know I only have minimum-wage jobs at an NGO available while I wait for openings at universities.'

'You are here on field work?'

'Yeah, a grant was approved for some cameras and more surveillance equipment, so I can finally start my field work early next year. I am here for a two-month recce.'

'Congratulations!'

'Thanks. I've asked for more money for better recording equipment though,' she said, taking another sip.

'I didn't know there were tigers here anymore,' mused Alice.

'But didn't you know? I am not working with tigers anymore.'

'Oh… What are you working on?'

'Forest areas attached to large urban settlements and metropolitan cities.'

'Ah … like the Guindy Park here?' asked Alice.

'Not just that. The marshlands and shrubbery too.'

'The dumping yards, you mean.'

'Yeah, exactly. It's horrifying, really, because they aren't just marshes, it's also supposed to be a bird sanctuary.'

'I am surprised the birds still come there. Why have you given up on tigers, though? I feel like I don't know you anymore.'

'Haha, I haven't given up on them. I am just studying habitats now.'

'Whatever helps you sleep at night.'

'Shut up. Are you still writing sports?'

'Oh fuck, I shouldn't have gotten so moralistic on you about tigers. No, I review books mostly now.'

'Well, well, well…'

'Freelance sports journalism is practically impossible, okay?'

'Whatever helps you sleep at night,' smirked Snigdha, nonchalantly pumping her fist. 'What kind of books, though?'

'Fiction, mostly. Whenever there's a graphic novel or a children's book by a popular writer. A couple of papers and a few websites.'

'No poetry?'

'Nope. Still don't get poetry. And I don't think there's any mainstream reviewing of poetry. A literary supplement or magazine maybe.'

'So you just do reviews now?'

'No, I do anything actually. Sports profiles, pop-science, even some civic politics, if it's trending. Some are commissioned. Some I write and sell. Reviews are the steadiest things I can do since I don't have the discipline for a column. Sometimes I act as a translator for white journalists. Those pay really well.'

'Must be exciting working with gori mems and tantalizing them with tales of the natives.'

'Haha, no such luck. Only sahebs and ABCDs.'

'That's really sad. Does it involve a lot of travelling?'

'Yeah, a little bit. Mostly around the four, now five, states. Train rides. Never beyond the peninsula, though.'

'So you are here now. Like Agastya.'

'Like Agastya. The Vindhyas can wait. Are you going to Delhi on this trip?'

'Maybe ... I don't know. My folks are with my brother in Australia. And Nani passed away a few years ago so...'

'Damn. I am really sorry to hear that.' Alice had met Snigdha's grandmother once and she had specially regained enough lucidity to remark that she found Alice very suspicious. It was the first coherent sentence she had spoken in months.

'So, if I have a lot of work here,' continued Snigdha, 'I might not go on this trip.'

'Don't. Stay here. Hang out with us. We could all go on a vacation.'

'Will Bakchod also come?'

'If the four of us are going, he will make it.'

'Sure?'

'For sure. He might be married and mellowed but always too much FOMO.' Alice laughed and drained the last of his drink.

Snigdha smiled. Her drink was almost over too. 'Has he changed a lot?' she enquired.

'I mean, I think so, and Nitin and Padma think so, but to be honest ... not so much. Not fundamentally. A tiger doesn't change its stripes.'

'Hmm... Can we order some food? I am really hungry.'

There weren't too many people at the bar, and the bartender, who was pretty much on standby, promptly took their orders, refilled their drinks and assured Snigdha he would soon be back with their food. The place was small— about ten small square tables and a kind of a community table at the centre. The furniture was tasteful but wasn't great or didn't stand out in any way. Alice and Snigdha scanned the other tables to see what the food looked like.

'We should have done this before ordering.' Alice smacked his forehead.

'That's okay, we can order more. What's that? That looks really nice.'

'That second table? With the couple? Some kind of platter.'

'Do you think they are married?'

Alice smiled. 'They are dressed too prettily.'

'So what?' countered Snigdha.

'This isn't the bar you'd have come to if you were married.' Alice had home turf advantage.

'Hmm ... their body language is pretty formal too,' agreed Snigdha.

'I'd say it's a first date.'

'Tinder?' she asked.

'Maybe they met somewhere,' offered Alice.

'So, two people clearly in their forties met organically and dolled up for a first date at this bar?' she scoffed.

'Okay, when you say it like that... Yeah, Tinder or equivalents. But, on a weekday?'

'Ooh, they like to live dangerously, don't they? Or maybe they're self-employed like us.'

'Maybe they have cushy corporate jobs. And they don't seem to be drinking much.'

'That's at least their fourth round. I've been trying to keep count,' said Snigdha.

'Whoa, they've been drinking the exact same thing?' exclaimed Alice.

'Hmm ... so?'

'Maybe they're regulars and they met here.'

'Too speculative,' Snigdha dismissed Alice's idea immediately. But in a few seconds she seemed to relent. 'It is curious, though, that they've been ordering the same thing. Is that something people normally do?'

'Maybe we should ask the bartender,' suggested Alice, taking a long sip of his drink and glowing in its warmth.

'Isn't he cute?' Snigdha giggled merrily.

'The bartender? Yeah, sure. Pretty good-looking. Really nice forearms.'

'Forearms? You've been looking at his forearms?' snorted Snigdha.

'Well, in the sense that he rolled up his sleeves and I could see his forearms and observe them in a socially admissible manner and say that they looked good?'

'What about them looked good?' teased Snigdha, still laughing.

Alice smiled to indicate he wasn't fazed. 'It was muscular and gleamy. And the hair seemed really soft. Not bristly.'

'Good observation. You'd make a good wingman,' she grinned.

'Do you want me to help you score with the bartender?' asked Alice.

'Maybe we'll come back again with that express agenda. Today, we'll just catch up.'

'Well said. You are a good friend. Ah, the food seems to have arrived.'

The bartender placed their dishes on the counter and proceeded to serve them in swift flowing motions. Snigdha cleared her throat. Alice wondered if she was going to flirt with him.

'If you don't mind ... do you know the couple at that table?' Snigdha pointed discreetly to the table. The bartender smiled a little but didn't betray surprise.

'The man comes often. His name is Venky. Works around here. Comes with friends usually. The woman...'

'The woman?' Alice asked unnecessarily.

The bartender continued politely, 'The woman's here for the first time. Never seen her before.' He finished serving, and smiling again, left.

'Wow!' exclaimed Alice softly. 'He didn't even ask us why we were being so curious about that couple. Very professional.'

'Yeah, and a little dangerous. So I guess it *is* a first Tinder-date kind of thing.'

'Seems that way. Do you want to order that platter?'

'Not really. I'll refill my drink, though.'

The food was decent. And even though it was on the higher side, the pricing wasn't extortionate. The naan was rubbery like all naans in the city, but the tikkas and gravy were quite tasty. Snigdha ate the tikkas with some kind of flavoured rice. The music wasn't good, but it had gone back to being played at a volume that was comfortable.

'So are you liking your work?' asked Alice, between mouthfuls of tikka.

Snigdha covered her mouth slightly to continue eating while talking. 'In principle, I love it. That's why I am doing my PhD on it. But in practice, it's really frustrating.'

'I think I remember you telling me about bureaucratic apathy or something like that.'

'Did I?' Snigdha laughed dryly. 'Oh, I was so naive. I wish it were apathy. But our forest department actually sees itself as a land and resource broker for mining and quarrying corporations. They are swiftly and efficiently fucking up.'

'Oh you know, I work on and off with a bunch of activists now. Write slogans, make posters, organize protests and that kind of stuff.'

'Oh my god! Me, too. Well, actually in my college, our whole department does, but still…' Snigdha finished the last of her rice and took a long sip of her drink. 'Did I tell you I learnt gimp?'

'Nice. Very cool. I have a really great book on protest art. I'll show it to you sometime.'

'Are you drunk enough? I feel like the setting really jars with our conversation. And the music is also getting progressively more dhik-chik.' Snigdha scowled.

'More than drunk enough. I barely drink these days,' slurred Alice, honestly.

'The roads would be empty right? Shall we just walk around?'

Snigdha paid the bill across the counter while Alice protested mildly and then walked towards the washrooms. The men's room was distinguished by a king of spades on the door while the women's room had a queen of hearts. The men's room was small and neat. Three urinals and two stalls. Alice looked at himself in the mirror and tried to adjust his hair. He was considerably drunk. He took a long and parabolic leak during which he tottered slightly due to a mild head rush. He washed his hand thoroughly, then rinsed his mouth. The bar hadn't offered any mouth freshener at the end of the meal. He took a little bit of the liquid soap and licked it. It smelt fresh but tasted soapy and medicinal. He licked some more and rinsed his mouth. The soap turned out to be unexpectedly frothy. It was so frothy Alice almost gagged on the froth while trying to spit it out.

Even though he spat all of it out in six or seven attempts, his subsequent rinses kept producing a lot of froth. After much more spitting and rinsing Alice pulled out a bunch of hand towels and wiped all of his mouth clean including the inside, and then checked himself thoroughly in the mirror for bits of paper in his beard or shirt before stepping out. Snigdha was already out and waiting for him.

'Which way shall we go?'

'You want to just wander about, right? ...I am not sure which way, I am really indecisive. Even more so when I am drunk.'

'Did you wash your face with soap?'

'Ummm … yeah. Just washed my beard. Summertime and all … gotta keep it clean.'

'Shall we walk in the direction of my guest house? It's less than two kilometres away.'

'Yeah, sounds good.'

By the time they stepped out of the restaurant, much of the traffic had subsided and the inner roads were quite empty. The air was still warm and humid, but there was the occasional breeze because there were hardly any high-rises around. Alice couldn't spot the moon. The streets were well-lit, and a few shops were still open.

Alice scratched the back of his neck and mused, 'You know … didn't think I would last till I was twenty-nine.'

Snigdha didn't say anything.

'Don't you turn thirty next month?' he prodded.

'Can we not talk about depressing things, Alice?'

'Haha, fair enough. So, this stretch we are walking on is the street parallel to one of the busiest markets.'

'Yeah, I've seen it and it's got an incredible number of jewellery shops. It's a mind-boggling number. I heard that people come from other states to buy jewellery for weddings.'

'People come from other countries to buy jewellery here. Especially the Gulf and South East.'

They took a left and decided to walk down a long road that wound into a blind left quite a distance away. Alice pointed to a few shops that he frequented and related a few anecdotes about his experiences in the area.

'You seem to have a lot of stories that involve cops,' observed Snigdha.

'Does it make me seem dangerous?'

'Mostly makes you look stupid. Whoa … wait … who are … are they?'

Alice could see the silhouettes of a group of women in the distance. As they came nearer, Alice realized that the silhouettes at the end of the road belonged to a group of four to five transgender extortionists. As they came still closer, he realized to his horror that another group was a little further behind them.

All of them wore sarees and two of them wore flowers in their sparse hair while the other three women had wound their tiny hair into knots with bright scrunchies. They clapped with glee and began to cry out in delight as soon as they spotted Alice and Snigdha. There were so many of them, Alice was sure they would empty both of their wallets out. He had a cheque coming in a few days, but he was down to his last hundreds in the bank account. So, he walked up to them confidently to negotiate. No sooner had he approached them than they all began to paw him. A couple of them played with Snigdha's hair and tried to grab her handbag.

'Akka, we are walking back home because neither of us has any money,' Alice offered before they could ask.

The women with flowers in their hair made exaggerated noises of disbelief, while their leader, the woman in red, with the purple hair and bald patch, pinched Alice's chin and said calmly, 'We can wait while you go to the ATM.'

'Making us do that is extortion. Please let us go,' Alice said, smiling sweetly. The youngest one in purple who was the most jovial of the lot, stopped playing with Snigdha's hair, came back up to Alice and said, 'Okay. We'll let you go if you give Akka a kiss.' She held Akka's face in her hands and turned her right cheek towards Alice.

Unperturbed, Alice replied, 'I'll kiss her, but you must make sure the group behind you doesn't bother us either.' The whisky was really good. He had been feeling strangely confident throughout the evening.

Thoroughly amused, they circled Alice and assured him with pats and mumbles that he had their word. Alice leaned over, hitched himself up on his toes and planted a long and firm kiss on Akka's cheek. The group erupted with joy, and hearing the commotion, the other group hurried nearer to find out what all the fuss was about. On hearing what had happened, they all shook hands with Alice and some of them hugged him and Snigdha. Then they all customarily blessed Alice and Snigdha before walking away, cackling delightedly. Snigdha and Alice bade them goodbye and took the left ahead of the large tree that had hidden the groups from Alice's view for so long.

'That was really sporting of you,' said Snigdha, grinning.

'You have no idea how broke I am.'

'Haha.'

'I pretty much fainted with relief back at the bar when you took the bill.'

'Don't worry, I can support us with my grant money while I am here.' Snigdha looked up at Alice and smiled.

He held her gaze and smiled back. She turned away and walked ahead. They walked in silence. There were a lot of questions begging to be answered, but they could wait for another day. For now, they had empty roads and trees and after-hour dosa stalls. They ate two dosas each in comfortable silence for a pittance that Alice paid for with an embarrassed chuckle and walked the rest of the way back to Snigdha's serviced guest house. She walked a couple of steps towards the rooms and then, all of a sudden, halted before climbing the stairs that led to her room, and said softly, 'We could go up to my room, but … no…'

Alice was a tad flummoxed. 'Will it be an issue?' he asked. 'We could—'

'It's just…' Snigdha interrupted. 'I want to sleep in your bed tonight.'

Alice smiled widely and grabbed her by the hand. 'Let's go,' he said.

'Will Nitin and Padma be awake?' she asked, while they turned around to head away from the guest house.

'No,' said Alice. 'Let's go. I'll book a cab.'

9

Javed's obsession with trying to understand the material reasons for the popularity of world religions began to yield results when he discovered a book that spoke about karma not just in terms of a system of spiritual merits and demerits but as a socio-economic system of debt and repayment. It spoke about all Axial Age world religions with a view to explain their popularity with the indebted classes of urban societies. It was a red book that Alice could never remember the name of.

'Do you know that the word for debt and the word for sin are the same in languages like Sanskrit, Aramaic and German?' Javed had asked, knowing fully well that Alice didn't. 'This is more or less true of most major languages that were popular during this time period. Frequent wars begot migrants and refugees, people dispossessed from their lands and religions, unable to call upon the help of sacred spirits that lived in their lakes and groves. They had to sell their labour for sustenance and any upheaval or even a festive occasion like marriage could send families into spirals of debt which would often end in slavery.

'The idea that a simple loan from a neighbour or local trust can result in slavery is outrageous. After all, what kind of neighbour or community would demand such a thing? Even if people were cruel, on what authority would a ruler or government enforce such repayment? This could only happen if the original debt itself was seen as a sin. The rulers were now free to rigidly enforce repayment even when repayment was not possible so that there would be a steady supply of debt peons for menial labour. Neighbours, too, found it simpler to look the other way while this happened, leading to an incredible amount of strain on social relationships in urban areas where kinship bonds were absent or very weak. This is an important context. We should remember this while talking about the rather deterministic philosophy of the Ajivikas.'

The Ajivikas didn't subscribe to the idea of karma. Instead, they believed that all events transpired as a web of three factors: Niyati, Sangati and Svabhava. Niyati represented the cosmic cause-effect cycle that began with time itself. Svabhava was the innate characteristics of the subjects and objects involved in the event. Sangati was serendipity or chance. Since this web of reality began with time itself, the Ajivikas believed that all events would unfold exactly as ordained. Their most important prophet, and later deity—Makkali Gosala—was represented as standing erect in meditation. Aware of everything but maintaining silent non-intervention. Silence was the most important abiding principle of the Ajivikas.

'To me this doesn't make sense,' Javed had said. 'Why would the working classes pray to a non-intervening deity especially when divine intervention is the one thing that can save them? Instead, it makes a lot more sense if Gosala is silent in non-judgement rather than non-intervention. A god or prophet who didn't see poverty as a sin and watched over people without judging them would have been a much more appealing prospect to an Axial Age wage labourer. Actions and consequences were not down to individual merits and demerits but due to cosmic factors and a good deal of luck. Socio-political and religious law that didn't see poverty as inherently sinful was truly revolutionary for the society that it emerged in.'

Even though Alice recalled the conversation, he didn't feel up to explaining all this to Snigdha. But still, since he had to, he explained it all very badly in a half-hearted fashion and said, 'The chapter where he challenges the idea that the Ajivika philosophy is deterministic is his most important contribution to the existing body of research. But it's also the most difficult to substantiate.'

'Yeah, I can imagine,' sighed Snigdha. 'It sounds incredibly speculative. And his reasoning feels a bit wishful. I can't really say without actually reading what he wrote but interpreting spiritual traditions in materialistic and especially economic terms has a really dicey colonial history. Even when it is done with solid evidence at hand, it arouses a lot of suspicion.'

'Hmmm, I should tell him that,' mused Alice. 'Or maybe I shouldn't. He's pretty fragile right now. He called me a few hours ago in the midst of a panic attack.'

'Poor guy,' tutted Snigdha. 'I don't know why people do PhDs and try to publish books. The whole process is inhuman and abusive.'

Alice smiled, comforted in the knowledge that even if he wanted to do a PhD no one would admit someone with his credentials into a programme. 'Masochism is a pretty dominant trait in people. Like we were just discussing, we are wired to interpret our punishing situations in life as punishment for sins. We tend to see suffering as noble in itself because suffering is how we cleanse ourselves of our sins.'

Alice was vegetating on the divan with his head on Snigdha's lap. Little munchie-mice were gnawing at his stomach, but it was still only a pleasant gnawing. Occasionally, Snigdha patted him on the head or ran her fingers through his hair and his stomach would purr in contentment. He was happy to wait for lunch as long as he could stay like that.

Snigdha curled a lock of his hair around her finger absent-mindedly. 'Let me remind you that I am not an ancient Indian wage-labourer. I suffer because I can see my work contributing to an important academic tradition.

Painstaking labour is the price of truth.' She smiled realizing she sounded a bit pompous.

Alice scoffed partly to tease her. 'I am sure those wage labourers also thought exactly that. Even as you suffer for your research, I am sure you tell yourself that you're just "paying your dues". By slaving away at a quarry, labourers would without a doubt have told themselves that they were contributing to an important architectural or religious tradition.'

'That's absurd,' countered Snigdha but didn't explain why. A few seconds later she said, 'It is strange, though, that people would come to see their existence and relationships in terms of debts and credits. Imagine thinking of a relationship as a network of debts? A kind of a marketplace of emotions and feelings. That's terrifying.'

'But that's also how we think. Not always but when push comes to shove we betray how we really think,' said Alice. 'Parents always talk to children about what is owed to them. In relationships we are constantly talking about what we owe each other. If not each other then we are told we owe something to the relationship itself. Even if we don't actively think this way, constantly stating it in terms of transactions has to have an impact on how we think about these things.'

Snigdha was about to respond when her stomach rumbled loudly. 'Nitin!' Alice yelled. Nitin peeped out of the kitchen. 'Yummy, yummy for my tummy,' Alice sang, patting Snigdha's stomach. 'Me, so hungry! Me, so hungry!'

Nitin's weekend lunches were simple but elaborately prepared, cooked only on low flame. Nitin entered his trance usually early in the morning before Alice woke up, cut the vegetables one at a time—not on a chopping board but literally in mid-air—into perfect shapes that dropped into the plate below, then continued to slowly grind spices and mix them in a precise order and quantity to make his masala. After that, Padma would come into the kitchen and put two glasses of rice and dal into the electric rice cooker. She would then head straight for the living room, collapse in exhaustion on the sofa there and watch some reality shows on Netflix while Nitin lovingly sautéed the onions, added the masalas, cooked the vegetables and prepared the dal. Then he would emerge from his trance to violently wake Alice up, who would, on quite a few occasions, be nursing a hangover.

But this weekend, Alice and Snigdha had woken up early in the morning to bake by the beach, watch the fishermen leave for their catch, and vegetate in the sun before it got too hot. They came back home much before Nitin had woken up and made the living room divan their nest, making and eating an inhuman number of butter, jam and cheese sandwiches, and then being dehydrated enough to not pee almost until noon. Alice daydreamed tirelessly while Snigdha flipped through some beauty magazine scoffing a number of times at every page. Why are you reading it if you hate it so much, Alice had wanted to ask, but desisted because, as his brain wisely pointed out, 'one's actions are only very rarely dictated by rationality'. His daydreams always made him feel zen. Then Snigdha was besieged by an urge to read something he had written, so he brought her his most recent article—one he was reasonably proud of. Still, she had picked out a hole in his argument. He was both embarrassed and slightly pleased with himself for being with her. That's how she made him feel most of the time, and it felt good. Maybe she likes being with you because your stupidity boosts her ego, his brain offered. Fine by me, thought Alice. He liked getting shown up by her. Somehow, with her, the embarrassment never rankled.

Nitin came out of the kitchen, drenched in sweat. 'I've put the lid on the sabzi,' he said, wiping himself with his red bawarchi shoulder towel and sitting next to Padma on the sofa. 'Let's watch.'

Snigdha readjusted Alice's head on her lap to a more comfortable position.

'It's so awesome that you guys have the AC in the living room,' she said.

'Yeah, it made more sense. We can't sleep with the AC on anyway because of my cold issues,' smiled Padma, turning the TV on. They had just begun watching some award winning-type American political drama that stunned Alice by how seriously it took its own clichés. Alice closed his eyes and tried to return to daydreaming, but following the dialogue in the show and trying to predict the next cliché turned out to be a much more compelling pastime.

By the time Nitin and Snigdha finished setting the table, Alice was ravenous. He dug into the food, adding a dollop of ghee to his rice. He had been eating Nitin's ghee for nearly a decade now but its taste still sent him into raptures.

'Listen, Nitin, if you have only one buffalo at home, how has it been giving birth to calves? There's some scandal there.'

'We can have the talk about how buffaloes get pregnant, but not at the lunch table,' answered Nitin, adding a considerable quantity of ghee to his own rice.

'Are buffalo calves also just called calves?' Alice turned to Snigdha. Snigdha was too busy demolishing her pile of rice. Alice added more dal to his rice. 'Buffies is a good name, no?' asked Alice. 'Buffies is cute.' But no one answered.

The rest of the lunch passed wordlessly. Alice and Snigdha ate twice as much as the other two, ensuring there were no leftovers. They had planned to go to a dessert shop that had just opened up, but everyone decided that a nap was in order and retired to their respective rooms.

Alice turned the fans on and collapsed on the bed. Snigdha snuggled up next to him and announced, 'I'm pretty horny, but I also can't move.'

'Yeah, I feel about the same way. Can you shift your head a little… Yeah … I am having dirty thoughts, but I am also totally flaccid. There seems to be no way to get around my packed stomach.'

'Hmm ... do you want to just sleep?'

'I do, Snigdha, but no! We can't be that couple. We are in the bubble.'

'So?' asked Snigdha, grinning and nuzzling his neck.

After spending the night at Alice's on the day they met, the question of what that meant and the future and other such questions inevitably popped up. While Alice fumbled, his fear of commitment battling his fear of missing out, Snigdha suggested that for the month and a half she had in her hands, they could be together in a kind of a 'bubble' where they didn't have to decide anything long-term until she came back for her year-long fieldwork. She didn't want to rush into anything so close on the heels of a break-up.

'So ... the bubble demands sex as sacrifice,' reasoned Alice. 'If we don't have sex, then we are just a regular couple. Like those two whose snores we can hear till here because they are so used to not having sex, they haven't even closed the door.'

'That's a pretty good point,' chuckled Snigdha, patting his cheek.

'How do we do this without moving at all?' asked Alice, gasping from the effort of talking.

'So, maybe, over the next five minutes we can just slowly take our pants off,' suggested Snigdha.

'Cool,' Alice agreed. 'And then we'll just lazily feel around until something clicks?'

'Yep. We have a pretty good plan.'

'This might just work.'

~

For Nitin and Padma, weekends meant something. Unlike Alice, they worked through the week and the two days of the weekend were reward for the dues they paid through the week.

They stole moments during hectic weekdays to elaborately plan their weekend in advance. Although they would ultimately only manage to do about half the things planned, the planning was nevertheless treasured activity and would always be loaded with ideas and suggestions they knew they would never get around to doing. The joy was, in fact, in just talking about it all together than in actually doing what they had spoken about. Alice was the same except he didn't have the structure of a week. He made plans in the morning he abandoned by evening.

However, since he had met Snigdha, he had been packing his days with cool things to do and actually found the drive to follow through with the plans. So much so that Snigdha came off looking like the laid-back one, occasionally cancelling plans to catch a breath. The bubble exempted Alice from thinking about the future and so he concentrated on the present with vigour. Everything that he couldn't be bothered to do by himself seemed like unmissable activities with Snigdha in the mix.

Nitin and Padma, who fretted over Alice's single status more than his own parents, were finally at peace. Alice often caught them smiling indulgently at him when he spoke about his plans with Snigdha or spoke to them about what they were up to. Presently, while Padma and Snigdha were getting ready for dinner, Nitin used the opportunity to have an adult man-to-man talk with Alice. As soon as both ladies retreated into Alice's room, Nitin went into the kitchen and emerged with two glasses of orange juice. He handed one glass to Alice.

'So, how is it going?' he asked. He sipped the juice like it was a mug of tea.

'Pretty fucking awesome.' Alice wiped some juice off his upper lip and smiled with satisfaction.

'So, is it official?'

'Is what ... Snigdha and me? No. We haven't spoken about anything.'

'What the hell, man? Don't make the same mistake you did last time. Do long distance or whatever, but make it work,' Nitin hissed, aiming to whisper but actually talking fairly loudly.

'No, no. Look, here's the thing,' Alice tried to explain, flailing his hands about. 'Think of what we are in as a bubble. The bubble has no past or future. It just exists while she is here for the next few weeks.'

'And then what?' asked Nitin disapprovingly.

'I don't know... We'll talk about it eventually, I guess.'

'I hope you know what you are doing?'

'No, I don't. But that's the point of the bubble. To not think about it while the bubble exists. The bubble shields me from such questions.'

'Okay, I won't ask any more questions … if that'll get you to stop saying "bubble".' Nitin sounded tired.

'Fine. But you know, I have been wondering if trying to figure out a more lasting relationship is actually a terrible idea,' said Alice, partly to annoy Nitin and partly because the thought was always at the back of his mind.

'That makes absolutely no sense.'

'Think about it. Maybe we are so good together because of the limited time we have had together. Think about Bakchod and Neha. Everyone thought they were really made for each other and perfectly compatible. What happened then? The years simply wore them out.'

'Listen, man. I don't know what you're up to. But just remember that you owe it to yourself to make it work this time,' said Nitin. Alice noticed that Nitin framed it as a debt to one's self.

The girls came out after fifteen minutes or so, wearing sarees. Padma wore one of her many kanjivaram cottons while Snigdha was draped in a blue and white ikkat that Padma had bought at a crafts fair recently. Nitin whistled while Alice hooted as the girls walked around showing off their pallus. After the hoots and applause subsided, Snigdha cleared her throat and said she had an announcement.

'Alice, since you've been showing me such amazing places, I've decided to surprise you with a visit to a place you've surprisingly never been to before.'

'What?' cried Alice, pretending to jump up in surprise. 'What is this place? Tell me, tell me.'

'No, I am taking you there,' said Snigdha. 'It's not that far. I was surprised when Padma said you guys hadn't been there.'

'Are you sure I don't know this place?' asked Alice, picking the keys up and leading them out of the door.

'Very sure,' nodded Padma.

Snigdha enjoyed driving Nitin's car. Compared to Delhi, the traffic in the city was a breeze. It was past eight and the office traffic, too, had subsided considerably. Snigdha pulled up at what seemed to be their destination in under fifteen minutes.

'I've been to this hotel and the bar a bunch of times,' Alice said to Padma.

'Not the hotel.'

'What else is here? The hospital? Actually, I've been there too—funny story…'

'Will you just shut up and follow Snigdha?'

Alice walked ahead and levelled up with Snigdha. He extended his arm and took her hand in his. She smiled but didn't look at him. She led him into the apartment complex adjoining the hospital. In a garage right at the entrance of the block was a small bookshop with a little, blue, hand-painted board announcing its name: Rare Bookshop.

'What the...!' exclaimed Alice. 'How did I not know about this place?'

'Yes!' Snigdha pumped her fist. 'I was surprised, too, but I am really really glad. A friend in the US is from here and she had recommended this place. So I had come here before I even met you.'

'This is amazing! It looks like he's just set up the bookshop in the garage.'

'Yeah, it's a twin garage. So there's enough space. What you can see now is only a part of it,' said Snigdha.

'This is most exciting!'

The bookshop was a clutter of old metal book racks creaking under the weight of old books, magazines and comics. The walls were dusty and adorned with artistic patterns formed by water seepage. The racks and the books on them were arranged in no particular order while the Mills and Boons, John Grishams and Tom Clancys were segregated into large bins. It was manned by an old man who looked rather annoyed at the arrival of the customers. Snigdha walked up to greet him.

'How are you, sir? All well?'

'You are back again? You took away some of my best illustrated weeklies,' he peered at her disapprovingly through his thick glasses.

'Oh, yes. They were really great editions. You have a treasure trove here!'

'Hmm... What are you looking for today?'

'My friends have never been here, so I thought I'll show them the place.'

'Sure, look around,' he turned to Alice. 'You won't find popular fiction here.'

'No, I really love old books.' Alice tried to look dignified despite his indignance.

Snigdha stifled a laugh and took Alice by the arm to the last rack, while Padma and Nitin browsed politely through the stack of folios on his table.

'Start looking around,' whispered Snigdha. 'He hides the best ones so people can't find them. He likes selling books but hates selling the really good ones.'

Alice's eyes swept over the stacks of books untidily arranged on the large metal shelves, his fidgety hands unable to settle on a book because all of them looked so inviting: edges frayed with age, moth-eaten pages and cloth bindings with golden block printed letters with the foil peeled off on several letters. 'Snigdha, can we never leave this place?'

'You know, if we steal the old man's glasses we can just hide in here and he'd never find us.'

The last rack had two metal props with five shelves each. Even here, the books were arranged in no particular order but magazines from the same country were heaped together in the corner of a random shelf. Alice began to pick out each book, systematically looking through its title and copyright page, chuckling at the dates and caressing the pages to feel

the indents of the blocks and the lovely classical shape of
the letters. He peered closely to observe how the ink traps
worked in block typography. The traps never ceased to
fascinate him.

There was a first edition Guy de Maupassant, its margins
filled with ink scribbles that had browned with age. They
weren't notes to the reading, they were jottings of things to
do, phone numbers and there was even a game of tic-tac-
toe. Alice loved books that had people's hurried scrawls
on them. Meera used to scan second-hand bookshops for
love notes and dedications. He remembered that he hadn't
replied to her last email or her WhatsApp message, but he
put it out of his mind. He was in the bubble. She would
understand.

There were a bunch of cookbooks on the third shelf and
one of them had lovely etchings of roasted chicken, cooked
fish, and even some of diced vegetables. As he was looking
through the drawings, Alice's eyes fell on a thin book
that was bound in black cloth and had a single gold stripe
running around its corners. He put the cookbook back in
and pulled the black book out and opened it.

'Snigdha! Look! It's *The Ajivikas* by B.M. Barua. This
is the first scholarly work ever written about the Ajivikas.'

'It's a rather thin book. But such lovely lettering.'

'Yeah, there isn't much information about them really.'

'It's in such good condition. And no one's even
scribbled in it.'

'You don't like scribbles?'

'My soul cries when I see that.'

'Haha. I didn't know that.'

'Why? Please don't tell me you scribble!' said Snigdha, eyes wide in somewhat genuine fear.

'I personally don't, but I love books with doodles or even highlights or notes on the margins.'

'What? How can you be a book lover and still be okay with such defacement?'

'One's defacement is another's adornment. It's like book graffiti. Is it art or vandalism?'

'Don't try to make this into a philosophical thing, okay? It's a disgusting habit.'

'Haha, okay.'

'But how come you don't write or doodle in books, then?'

'I got such a legendary thrashing from my mum when I did it as a kid. My hands still can't hold a pen near printed material.'

'That is amazing parenting. If there were a Nobel for parenting, your mother would get it,' said Snigdha.

'I am obviously taking this,' Alice said, staring lovingly at the book. 'This place is just amazing!'

They scanned some more shelves, picking out books until Nitin peeked in, tapping on his watch. They both proudly carried their haul out and set it on the desk. The old man looked at all the books.

'There's no fixed price. I'll look at the books and decide how much I want to charge.'

Alice nodded smartly. He didn't really care. He was already in debt and could afford a little more debt. Eventually, the articles he would write about the bookshop would pay for the books, he comforted himself.

The old man began to open each book, pause thoughtfully, and then write down the cost on a little scribble pad he had on his desk. The blunt pencil made barely visible markings on the paper, but Alice could see that the man wasn't charging more than a hundred-odd rupees for any of the books.

'*Corporate Life in Ancient India* by R.C. Majumdar,' he read the title out loud. 'Where did you find this?'

'In the last row. In one of the upper shelves, I think.'

'There must be a mistake. This book is not for sale. It's a very old book. It's a textbook, actually. What would you want with it anyway?'

'I am interested in history, sir,' Alice ignored the barb again with some difficulty.

'All the same, I am sorry. This book is not for sale.'

'Oh, okay. That's all right, I guess.'

'You see, these books are not easy to come by. I only sell books so that I can make enough money to buy more.'

'That's a great model. I hope I'll be able to do that someday.'

'I have some great old comic books as well. Are you sure you don't want those? Some Phantoms, Mandrakes and Tarzans.'

'Yeah, my friend has picked them up. I'll just take these.' Nitin's arms were bursting with comic books.

The old man tallied all the books and the four paid for all of them. He even grumbled about losing change and rounded the costs off to increase them, perhaps hoping they would refuse to buy the books. They all picked up their books and were about to make their exit when the owner called Alice back.

'What will you do with this book?' he asked Alice, holding up the book he had confiscated.

'I'll read it, sir.'

'It would be quite boring.'

'I'll find it interesting, sir. Life is very boring.'

'Okay, but I can't just give this away. It's a very rare and precious book. I am only giving it to you because I have so many more books to read that I'll never get to this.'

'Of course.'

'I am going to charge a bomb for this.'

'Sure, no problem.'

He wrote the numbers 2-5-0 down on his scribble pad. Alice wanted to laugh. Instead, he gladly handed the money to the old man, thanked him profusely while shaking his hand, and walked away pleased as punch.

～

The sky was cloudy and almost all the lights in the fishing hamlet and the town around had been turned off. The moon was tucked away in a corner shining its meagre light on a lone tanker ship in the horizon while the rest of the sky shimmered in patches along with the sea beneath it. The sand, unmolested for the last few hours and smoothened by the sea's caresses, lay pristine and seemed irresistible to Snigdha, who dangled her feet expectantly from a large rock on the beach.

'You can't make me wait like this for my special present that's supposed to make up for seven years' worth of birthdays.'

'The charm is in the longing and the waiting.' Alice tried to sound profound, sitting cross-legged next to her.

'You can't be thinking of showing me turtle nests because it's too late in the year for that.'

'Nope. I know you've been on a turtle walk before.'

'We've been here for an hour. Can I get on the sand now?' Snigdha's hair was repeatedly getting tangled in her glasses. She took them off and hung them around her neck.

'Wait. Let me build this up. I can't just let you do it. I need to say something that's poignant but that also has a lot of veiled romance.' Alice smiled, enjoying the breeze against his newly shaved cheeks.

'Okay, now you can't say anything because you've ruined whatever you might have said by explaining it. So, now can I walk?'

'Yes. But as much as I enjoy your deepening cleavage, you'll need to put your glasses back on for this.'

Snigdha, bespectacled again, jumped softly on to the sand and took a few tentative steps and, as she walked, the sand around her feet began to shimmer and glow.

'Get the fuck out of here!' she gasped. Everywhere she stepped, the sand began to glitter.

'It's amazing, right?' Alice smiled smugly. He was getting the reaction he was hoping for.

Snigdha hopped around a few times, the sand all around her feet beginning to glimmer like fireflies. 'Bioluminescent plankton!' she whispered.

'What the hell!' groaned Alice, disappointed. 'You know what they are?'

'Oh, no. Don't be disappointed. This is really amazing. I've only ever heard of them. So this is really special.'

Alice and Snigdha were on the beach of a fishing town outside the city. Snigdha had told him that she wanted to see the city through his eyes. So, after taking her around on an elevated rail one day and then to the salt pans near the creek on another, this was to be his coup de grâce. His trump card. The perfect trilogy.

She walked up, cupped his faced in her hands and kissed him tenderly at first and then with a fierce passion, making him see stars everywhere he looked. She let go of his face after a long time, but continued to look deeply into his eyes.

'This is the most beautiful thing I have ever seen. Thank you. Come down. Walk with me.'

Snigdha pulled Alice by the hand. They walked towards the water, arms around each other's waists, looking down at the stars beneath their feet.

'It's like glitter everywhere we put our feet on instead of sand.' She scooped up some sand in her palms. Under the light of their phones, they could see some translucent jelly that generated sparks of electricity. They let it dissolve in the foam of a receding wave. On the next wave, Snigdha gently washed the sand off her hands and leaned against a large rock. Alice turned to her and, brushing some hair off her face, tucked it behind her ear.

'Now that I've seen this place through your eyes, I can tell why you never leave this city.'

'Trust me, I really want to,' Alice replied and laughed. 'But it's a "Hotel California" sort of a situation.'

'Sounds a lot like my PhD.' Snigdha laughed. 'We really are just prisoners of our own device.'

'I can't believe you aren't working on tigers, though. Like, you just gave up on them,' said Alice.

Snigdha groaned. 'God! I didn't give up on them. I still work to protect habitats. I think the connection is pretty obvious, right. I now work to create spaces where all wildlife can thrive,' Snigdha clarified.

'But it's not tigers. I mean who cares about lizards, rodents and insects, right?'

'Haha, you know that's a hot topic in conservation right now. Overemphasis on conserving cute animals.'

'Tigers aren't cute! Tigers are...' Alice flexed his arms and tightened his fingers in a hook to try and mime strength and majesty. 'In the absence of unicorns, tigers are all we have.'

'*Okay!* ... I'll be sure to include that statement in my thesis. Makes more sense than whatever I've written so far,' Snigdha grinned. 'I thought I was passionate about something and I thought it would last a lifetime, but life is both really short and really long, I guess.'

'Yeah, it is weird how fundamentally I have changed in these last seven years. I don't even have the same name anymore.'

'No one calls you Alice?'

'Only Nitin and Padma. Now, you.'

'Hmm ... I feel like back then, I was so sure of things. I think after sixteen your brain is able to process so much information that by twenty-two you are sure that you are at the cusp of a major revelation,' Snigdha sighed. 'But the revelation never comes. You ride the cusp through your twenties and then you realize that that feeling is your carrot and stick. That feeling is all there is, and you need to make it last a lifetime. There's no revelation on the other side.'

'Wow, yeah. I couldn't have put it better myself. Except for me, it was never finding the passion and just directly jumping into the abyss.'

'You jump into the abyss and the abyss jumps right back into you.'

'Haha. Yeah. I think I am past the age where I can define myself by my work even if I found such work. At that point I was trying to find an identity. But I don't think "need" is relevant to me anymore.'

'You can still define yourself by multiple things. Your identity doesn't have to be one thing.'

'No, of course not, but that's not what I am talking about. See, identity is about defining yourself either to other people or to your own self, right? That has really ceased to be interesting.'

'So, what drives your existential crises these days?'

'Haha. That was a devastatingly well-framed question. Hmmmm … so you remember how in *Scrubs*, J.D. calls himself a self-saboteur?'

Snigdha burst out laughing. 'Oh god, yes! He's hilarious. And yes, you are a classic self-saboteur!'

'Exactly, I was always a self-saboteur in my daily life and everyday interactions. But now I am able to like, you know, really, feel it at, like, an experiential level.'

Snigdha doubled up with laughter. 'The fuck's that supposed to mean?'

Alice grinned stupidly and tried to find the words. The waves were now consistently ankle high. Alice was wearing shorts and Snigdha had hitched her cotton pants well above her knees. A large fluffy cloud that looked like a teddy bear in the far corner of the sky had now travelled a considerable distance and looked more like a hippo's butt that had just pooped out the moon.

'I don't know.' Alice scratched the back of his neck. 'Like when we were growing up, it was like a commonly held social belief that we are supposed to think rationally? To develop this problem-solving attitude. That's still the basis of all of our competitive exams. IIT or IAS or CAT or whatever. We were all taught to think that way and aspire to refine that thought process.'

'But we are not fundamentally rational people...'

'Yeah, but that's not what I am getting at. I am talking about what aspiring to that kind of thinking does to our brain. Right now our brain is taught to start from the problem and just find the shortest, most efficient route to the solution. Like an express highway from problem to solution, that cuts through villages and marshlands and elephant corridors and tiger reserves...'

'I like the analogy.' Snigdha kissed him.

'Thank you... That's exactly why your bureaucrats come up with and approve of such plans, right? Because they are the best in the whole country at thinking in this fucked-up way. There's urgency and efficiency but there's no harmony or justice.' Alice paused. 'And at an individual level, it has fucked up my thinking. My experiences are being catalogued for efficiency so that everything just starts vaguely resembling everything else. A copy of a copy of a copy.'

'See I agree that's like a perfect rant to get into my pants. It makes you look broody and mysterious, and it's got my politics,' Snigdha chuckled.

'Thank you. I am glad, because everything I say to you is said with the intention of getting into your pants.'

Snigdha grinned impishly. 'There's a but.'

'Oh … there's a "but"? What's the "but"?'

'But … I wonder if you are attributing cause to your feelings. Maybe you are looking at this whole thing backwards. What about the fact that you are consciously limiting your experiences? You haven't travelled around the world, you haven't been married or had children. You haven't really pushed yourself, have you?'

'Yes, I've also not smuggled drugs or committed genocide. God, don't be so literal. I am talking about the feeling of experiencing. I think I am just doing a very bad job of explaining. Let me try and tell you the genesis of this thought. I was visiting Javed before he had his…'

'Why am I not surprised? Everything weird and loopy in your life ties back to Javed, one way or another. If I hadn't actually met him, I would have thought he was just like a split-personality that was the expression of your superego or something.'

'Well, he does have a superego. But this also ties into the Ajivika philosophy.'

'Oh goody! Do tell.' Snigdha laughed, turning around to walk back towards the rocks. Alice took her hand in his and softly stroked her thumb with his. 'No,' he said, 'some other time may be. We can't be those guys who come to the beach in the middle of the night and talk about Javed and his book.'

'The bubble demands sacrifice.'

'Exactly. God! You are so quick to learn,' Alice tried to put on his sexy voice.

'I am learning from the best,' Snigdha giggled.

He took her by the waist and led her towards the wet sand. Crabs ran out of their holes and scurried into ones farther away. Snigdha played a jazz mix on her music app. The first song was '*Mahi Ve*' by a Pakistani pop star whose name he couldn't remember presently. In the moonlight, the waves appeared black and white, like the shifting dunes on a desert studded with diamonds. Alice and Snigdha kissed and danced into midnight talking about the stars, the moon, the sky, and everything under it. They spoke about everything except for how they saw each other figuring in their own futures.

10

Over the last few years, Alice had begun to imagine his life, more and more frequently, as a TV show. His show always played out in front of a live audience. Being single, predictably, his most significant subconscious anxiety was the absence of a partner who could serve as a chronicler. So, the audience, as witness, had always been very important.

What had started off as a nice, peppy, coming-of-age sitcom in his late teens and early twenties had gradually morphed into a dreary slice-of-life web series. A four-camera set-up became one with a single camera, while OSTs and voice-over narration made the studio audience obsolete. The writing team was replaced by a YouTube stand-up comedian who had that one viral set that was rather more topical than funny. The comedian was floundering. The scripts were dreary and plots predictable. There was no originality because imagination was essentially dying.

And then the comedian, deciding to make one last desperate attempt, to prove more to himself than anyone else that he is the master of his script, brings back a popular character from the protagonist's past. He had been foolish to have written her out in the first place.

The ploy seems to work. The press warms up to the twist, and subsequently, the audience lap up the romance. But the ploy had worked because of the bubble. Sooner or later, the comedian will have to bring things to a head. The bubble will have to burst.

As soon as Alice saw a number from the United States flash on Snigdha's phone on the morning of her departure, he realized this was that moment. She was all packed, and they still had a ton of things to do that day. The bubble was about to officially end but they were just prolonging it by rolling around in bed, holding their bodies together to make memories. It was languorous and sensuous but that was a perfect set-up to make the burst of the bubble more impactful.

Ta-da! The popular character's never-before-referenced ex-boyfriend calls her out of the blue. It is bad writing; but that is all our comedian is really capable of.

For some reason, Snigdha put her clothes on before she answered the phone. Alice wondered if he should leave the room, but as though reading his thoughts, Snigdha said, 'Stay.' And then she walked away to look out of the window.

Throughout the call, which was barely ten minutes long, Snigdha mostly only said 'hmm' or 'no'. Occasionally she said, 'Maybe to you.' Alice took his phone out to text someone or reply to mails but ended up just staring at the screen while his mind drifted to the various reasons as to why they might have broken up.

Maybe he had cheated on her. She was being curt and had her poker face on. Maybe she wants to get married but he keeps putting it off. Did he call to propose to her? Whoa, it would be so hilarious, trilled his brain, if he does propose and she says yes, and you are just sitting here watching them in your underwear. He put his clothes on immediately.

But it didn't look like any proposal was forthcoming in the next few minutes, so he wondered if she had maybe found out he was already married. Padma did mention it was an older guy. In Alice's imagination he was variously forty years old, fifty years old and bizarrely, sometimes, in his late seventies or eighties. Snigdha had done a marvellous job of existing in the bubble. She never mentioned him; she hardly ever spoke about her time abroad. And Alice hadn't asked either. It really was like no time had elapsed.

Maybe he had given her a venereal disease, his brain suggested, unhelpfully. But she would have told him about that, he hoped. Most probably, he, Alice, was overthinking it. Perhaps it was 'some more humble lay, familiar matter of today'. Maybe he was inattentive, or she was just bored. Maybe it was time that had taken its toll.

He had been thinking about what Nitin had said. Maybe that's what adulthood was. The need for a stable place to rest. A decision to root your journey in one place.

But that wasn't for everyone. Did Alice want a long-term relationship with Snigdha?

It really wasn't in his hands anyway. He had to see how this would play out. Snigdha had her famed poker face on and she was at her monosyllabic best. Just as he thought that it looked like the conversation would go on much longer, she cut the call and flung her phone aside on to his study desk. She collapsed dramatically on to the bed and searched for Alice's lap.

'So…?' asked Alice, smiling, helping her coax her head on to his thigh.

'You never asked me anything about my relationship…' said Snigdha, settling in.

'Yeah, you know, because of the bubble and all … I thought you'd tell me about it later. And honestly, also because I wasn't really curious.'

'Not at all curious?'

'Well, curious, but limited to his role in how things pan out for us.'

Snigdha sat up on the bed and readjusted her T-shirt.

'As you might have guessed, he was calling to try and patch things up.'

Alice didn't really want to know but it had come to a point where he had to ask. 'Why did you break up? Actually, come to think of it, I don't know his name. Start with that.'

'Haha. Okay, his name is Matthew. He's also a grad student, but in a different department. It's his second PhD.'

'See, people are inherently masochistic!' Alice laughed. 'So why did you break up?'

'At this point, it's a really complex matrix of who did what, when, because of what. We've been together for almost four years now. It's really confusing even to me.'

Alice noticed the use of the present tense but didn't mention it. 'How do you feel after talking to him? You can be honest with me.'

'I don't know. I think I feel like I am really ready to move on.'

'Are you sure?'

'Yeah. I feel really sure. But I really wish I didn't have to go back, though. A lot of my stuff is still over at his place, and judging by this phone call, it doesn't look like he's going to make it very easy for me.'

'Hey maybe I can call and threaten him.'

Snigdha laughed but didn't reply. Instead, she said, 'You know, I've often thought about what it would be like if we didn't break up when I left.'

'Oh, man! Me, too,' he said softly. 'So many times.'

'Do you remember why we broke up, though?' asked Snigdha.

'You know, I can't really remember. I have a lot of reasons I have come up with in hindsight, but I don't know,' Alice replied, unsure what to say.

'I remember really panicking,' said Snigdha. 'I could have deferred my admission by a year, I could have suggested long distance, but I think at that point I just wanted to leave.'

Alice was caught by surprise. He expected Snigdha to say something accusatory about him not taking initiative. He didn't realize she had taken the call to break up. He remembered the whole thing so differently.

'Do you remember what we spoke about?' he asked softly.

'You said something about preserving what was perfect. I thought it was really beautiful. I remember crying a lot. You were trying to comfort me, but I didn't really hear what you said.'

'Nothing profound I am sure,' said Alice, smiling. 'I remember crying too and being perplexed about why exactly I was crying. But I also remember thinking I'd see you in a couple of years at the most. That our paths would cross much sooner. In the digital age, especially!'

'I didn't think it would be seven years either.'

'I am old, Snigdha. The bubble was just an adrenaline rush. My insides are rotting.'

Snigdha laughed and hugged Alice tightly. 'Have you ever wondered, though, if we are so good together only because we've had limited time? We've never gone past the honeymoon phase.'

So she had thought about it too. Alice stroked her arm gently. 'Yeah, of course. I, too, have thought about that. But I've not even been able to work a relationship through the honeymoon phase ever since, so it is still significant to me.'

'That's because you are still a child.' She didn't sound irritated. She just stated it.

'I feel there is a secret to growing up that I am not privy to,' he smiled.

'Which is why this was perfect for two months, but I don't see how we can keep this up even for four years, as I have with Matthew, leave alone for life.'

'Listen, I know I need to change too. I don't want to be this way. And I promise things will be different. I've given this a lot of thought and I really think I am ready. Okay, I don't think I am ready, but I am supposed to be ready, so I am effectively ready for the plunge. Haha.'

Snigdha sighed and smiled a little. 'Alice, I don't know how to tell you this, but overseeing a boy's transition to adulthood through his thirties is no girl's dream.'

'No, of course not. I didn't mean it that way … no, I think you are right. This was good while it lasted. But … in the long run … you deserve better, Snigdha. I do want that for you, even though I don't really feel that way right now.' Alice probably looked miserable because, all of a sudden, Snigdha's face had softened. She took his face in her hands and kissed him softly several times.

'I think this was a really bad time for us to have this conversation. Matthew's call put me off and I am a little anxious about all the things I need to do before the flight. We can text, call and video call whenever we want to. We'll figure this out. I want to make it work.'

'Sure,' Alice replied with a smile. 'We can talk this over long, unending conversations, like adults.'

'Like adults.' Snigdha smiled back.

This would be a good time for a soft ambiguous ending, but Alice's show didn't have episodes that ended anywhere. Like an art filmmaker's graduation thesis, they just went on and on and on. Snigdha and Alice got dressed and went out to the kitchen to lunch with Nitin, Padma, Chikki, Anu and DB, who had all come to say goodbye to her.

~

On his way back from the airport, Alice picked up Bhaskar from the recording studio thanks to a new feature on his taxi app that allowed him to add pickup points on his ride. Bhaskar appeared tired but seemed really excited about the new song he was working on.

'See, the lyrics are really abstract,' he started off as soon as he settled in his seat. 'What I am trying to say is really ambitious I guess. But the same ambition needs to translate to the music.'

'Which song is this one, again?' asked Alice. Bhaskar was working on at least six different songs at any point of time.

'The beach song.'

'Ah okay.' Alice yawned. He was tired from running around with the luggage trolley. 'I don't really understand that song.'

'Well, yeah…' Bhaskar agreed, 'which is why I need the music to obviate the subtext.'

'Your song has subtext? I don't think that's a very good idea. I hate songs with subtext. The beach song shouldn't have subtext. What subtext can be there for a beach song?'

Bhaskar was unfazed by the criticism. 'Essentially this. Look, we all seem to think that our current social situation is a deviation from the ideal. The ideal is defined by this period of time in the distant past where and when justice was realized.'

'But the ideal is imaginary.' Alice knew this rant. 'Such a time had never actually existed.'

'Exactly. That's the first chorus. The second stanza and its chorus are about this: if the ideal is imaginary and had never been realized in the past, then our current social situation is not a deviation at all! It is actually a march towards this ideal. It's not a fall from grace, it's an inspirational journey.'

'Ah nice!' grinned Alice. 'I like that. Nice little twist. Very you, I must say.'

'Thanks.' Bhaskar smiled.

'What's the bridge?'

'I am a little conflicted on the bridge. It should say that justice is a historical inevitability and anyone who stands against it will ... ummm ... die or burn or ... I don't know man. Something shitty will happen to shitty people who stand against justice. That's what it should say.'

'Have you written anything?' asked Alice, rolling the window down to look outside. They were almost home.

'I've written the ideas down, but I don't have the words yet,' mumbled Bhaskar.

While climbing up the stairs, Bhaskar exclaimed suddenly, 'I forgot to ask! How are you? Has she left?'

'Her flight will take off in an hour or so,' replied Alice, looking at the time on his phone. 'I am fine. I am just feeling bummed out that I don't have any more excuses to put off work.'

They walked down the corridor to Anu's house and rang the bell. As soon as she opened the door, Bhaskar made a beeline for Anu's bedroom, turned the AC on and collapsed on the bed in exhaustion.

Alice took a water bottle out of the fridge and settled in the bean bag in the living room, moving it right under the fan and also next to the window.

'I am drenched in sweat after walking up one floor,' he complained to Anu between gulps of cold water. She sat on the floor with her back resting against the sofa.

'Straight from the airport?' she asked.

'Yeah … flight's in an hour.' Alice felt like it was ages since he had hung out with Anu.

'So, are you guys going to do long-distance, or…'

'No, I don't even know if she's really out of her old relationship.'

'What!' exclaimed Anu. 'But she called him her ex just earlier at lunch.'

'Yeah, but she also referred to their relationship in the present tense.'

'Ouch. Yeah, Freudian slips are the worst.' Anu scowled. 'But maybe it was just force of habit, you know.'

'Maybe,' said Alice. But he was also thinking about the fact that she was the one who had ended it the previous time. 'I don't know. I'm not fussed, though,' he said somewhat sincerely. 'Maybe we are good just in these short intense bursts. We aren't meant to have a traditional long-term relationship.'

Anu reached for the bottle of water and wiped off the condensation on the floor with a tissue from the coffee table. She sipped from the bottle a few times pensively.

'You remember I was a little weird for a week or so after…'

'I am so sorry, Anu,' said Alice gravely, cutting her off. 'When I met Snigdha, I had no idea. And when it happened, I couldn't…'

Anu smiled. 'I get it,' she said. 'Anyway it's not like we were in a relationship.'

'But it was … something. And Snigdha and I didn't really talk about a relationship either. Which is why I was so vague in that message.'

'It's all right. What I mean to say is that although it was weird for me the first one week,' Anu continued, 'it's not like we were in a relationship. So I got over it and then it was actually cathartic in a way. I felt that maybe I was being so cautious I had stopped having a life.'

'I am known to inspire people in unexpected ways,' said Alice, smiling.

Anu chuckled. 'I was actually rooting for you guys to get together. It would have, sort of, helped with my affirmations. I am trying to get back in the game myself.'

'Whooaa,' Alice hooted. 'Who's the lucky boy?'

'I mean we aren't officially going out or anything but we've had a few good dates.'

'Fine, fine … but who's the guy?' asked Alice impatiently.

'You remember that guy at Bhaskar's midnight recording?'

'No! Not him. Not Pretty Boy!'

'Can you please hear me out?'

'God, Anu! Why him? I'm sure he's like a total fuckboi, I could smell it from the street. Anybody but him. Please. Just anyone!'

Anu closed her ears with her palms while laughing and yelled, 'Will you please just hear me out?'

Alice caught her hands and pulled them away from her ears. 'Fine, fine. Tell me. I just wanted to register my protest.'

'You don't even know him.'

'I know the type.'

'I was a little upset with the whole Snigdha thing and so … I called him.'

'God. I didn't know my thing with Snigdha would result in such tragic consequences for you. Now I am even more sorry.'

Anu laughed. 'Anyway ... he called me over for a house party. I almost didn't go but I am really glad I did, because I met someone there.'

'So, not Pretty Boy?'

'No. His college friend Kamesh. I was very very drunk and he was really sweet and funny. We both slipped in our single status in this really obvious and corny way, so it was sort of out there.'

Alice didn't know how he felt about it, exactly, but he was happy for Anu. 'So how come you guys aren't going out yet?'

'I've been busy with the ad-shoot, so we've only met a few times since. He's a software engineer with some tech firm, so he's free only on the weekends.'

'Techie? Really?'

'Hey! Techies are people too, okay!'

'Hmm ... maybe.'

'He's geeky but also kind of an old-school romantic. We have amazing conversations, and when we met day before, we held hands for a while.'

'Go, wash your mouth. That's dirty!' mocked Alice.

'Shut up. It was really romantic. Anyway, he's coming over for dinner. This weekend, we are doing it for sure,' Anu winked.

'Okay, too much information. This ... you and me ... it's still weird. We need to have boundaries.'

'Snigdha and you were having sex while I waited in the living room for lunch,' Anu said accusingly.

'What?! No. That wasn't … we … her ex had called. She was talking to him. I was just waiting … sexlessly … no sex.'

'Oh! Her ex called? What did they talk about?' Anu had her gossip-face on. She couldn't resist gossip. That was a major reason why she enjoyed being in the film industry.

'Apparently, he was trying to get back together with her. And now she has to go back there to pack her stuff while he tries to grope her or whatever,' rambled Alice angrily.

'And you feel she might want to get back together too?' asked Anu.

'Yeah. She didn't seem to have a serious reason not to be with him. And they've been together four years.'

'What?' gasped Anu. 'Four years! Fuck. That's like … I don't know … eight or ten relationships for me.'

Alice laughed. 'Yeah. She's the nesting type, I guess. I think we are different people, except we've never been together long enough for that to become an issue.'

'I don't know … Nitin and Padma seem to think you guys are just made for each other. And you are really cute together. Her quiet self-confidence and your complete cluelessness. It might work.'

'I do believe that smart girls can't resist a charity case, so I'll remain slightly hopeful I guess,' laughed Alice, pointing at her. 'But honestly, any human being would expect some clarity on the future. I, however, am just not programmed to think far ahead.'

'I know you have a lot going on right now, but you won't always. Or you'll get tired of this. A long-term relationship might be scary but it's also a sort of investment. A kind of a compromise we can strike because we are blessed with the ability to think ahead.'

'Yeah, that's also true,' mused Alice. 'Should I make overt gestures to underscore my intent with her?'

'Yes, court her. Serenade her,' said Anu, smilingly.

'Maybe I will.' Alice smiled back. 'Maybe I will.'

~

Alice typed his name and clicked send.

He put his laptop away and crawled up to the pillows and rested his back against the curved plywood headstand.

He pulled his phone out and called Chikki. The phone rang several times, but she didn't pick up. Bhaskar was still asleep at Anu's and Anu was out, presumably with Kamesh. Nitin and Padma wouldn't drink because it was a weekday. He felt there was just too much on his mind and he needed to talk a lot before he could even figure anything out. He wished it was possible in India to just talk to a bartender. But still, he would have to wrap up not long after eleven, thanks to ridiculous bar timings.

After a while he decided that he was finally bored enough to call Javed and had also read enough of the chapter to navigate his way through a conversation. He called, and much to Alice's irritation, Javed connected the call and sent a video request. Alice grumbled for a few seconds but gave in.

'Why this sudden urge to see my face?' asked Alice as soon as the connection stabilized and they could see and hear each other.

'Cutting vegetables,' Javed replied. Chhotu, who now had a wife and two kids, had been teaching him to cook.

'Hmmm... So, you finally decided to call. I am assuming whatshername has gone back to wherever and so blood has started flowing back to your brain.'

'This is a pity call, okay. I feel bad about what you're putting yourself through for something as pointless as a burning life ambition. Tut, tut.'

'I guess I was wrong about the blood returning to the brain. Anyway, I hope you called because you finally read the whole chapter.'

'Well, yeah. More or less,' answered Alice, truthfully. 'I am intrigued by what you say while wondering if you really have enough to substantiate what you're saying. Like one thing really caught my attention. I was talking to Snigdha about it too. You said that most philosophers of the age, including people like Socrates, thought about life in terms of debts we owe to each other and to society.'

'Well, we all still think that way. Like it says here,' Javed raised the red book making Alice wonder why it was next to him in the kitchen. '"Most horrific things like selling women and children to repay debts or asking young men and women to die in pointless wars were and sometimes still are all justified by framing it in the language of what we owe each other or what we owe our society at large. Repayment of debts is considered the most important virtue and non-repayment, consequently, is the greatest imaginable sin. It's called debt-morality.'"

'Hmmm … I should read that book sometime I guess,' said Alice for the millionth time in the last five years.

'You should. The author literally shows how we are all just so used to thinking of everything on these terms that we have forgotten that there are other ways to look at life and what gives it purpose. It's like we are in this thought matrix. Things seem a certain way because we live in this matrix, this kind of thinking. But if we stop thinking in the language and logic of debt morality, the whole world appears completely different and you gain access to a kind of freedom that makes you realize what you thought was freedom was not freedom at all.'

'Wow. Okay. That's really interesting,' admitted Alice. 'The whole idea that we are in a thought matrix that is imprisoning us is gold. This is the kind of stuff that forms the basis of an international grade spiritual franchise.'

'Oh my god, shut the fuck up,' Javed groaned, but Alice was not deterred.

'Who is this author? Does he have his own cult?' Alice asked.

'He's an economist and anthropologist. He's taught at places like Yale and London School of Economics. He's talking about serious stuff.'

'Well, yes. Spirituality is serious,' said Alice condescendingly. 'The Church of Ajivikism is serious stuff. You know, having academic credentials is not necessarily a bad thing in a godman as long as you know how to spin it. Like you have all this knowledge, but you should also emphasize how you found scientific and academic knowledge systems limiting and how you are helping people aspire to something higher.'

'Just shut up and tell me what you thought of the chapter,' hissed Javed.

'It's good. And also, it's as good as it will ever get. Your issues aren't going to get magically resolved unless there is a sudden discovery of lost Ajivika scriptures that completely substantiate what you're saying. You know it'll court controversy. Your editor has made peace with it. So you should make peace with it as well.'

'Does it sound really weak?'

'Compared to the thought matrix stuff you just tried to sell me, what you wrote in your chapter sounds far more grounded and reasonable. But seriously you are adding literature to and reviving conversation about a topic where the trail is widely assumed to have gone cold. That should be enough in and of itself.'

'Hmmm. Thanks for saying that. I keep telling myself that but it's good to hear somebody else say it too. My editor has just given up on me at this point. He just wants me to be done. He's really unhelpful.'

Alice listened patiently while Javed whined about his editor. Alice was tempted to say "You know, Javed, there are two kinds of insane people in this world: science types and arts types. The science types are curious about how things are and what makes them tick. They'll do anything to dig up facts. The arts types don't care so much about how things are. They are more focused on how things should be. If I know anything about you it is that you are the kind of person who feels really strongly about how things should be. But you are pigeonholing yourself into a kind of research that forces you to focus on how things really were. Fuck that shit. Just write about how things should be. So just finish this book. However it is. And then get back to cooking up a revolution. The world doesn't need analyses. It needs action.

"If people like you don't do it, then it'll be down to people like me which is why you see so many godmen, spiritual gurus and mystical masters with their luxury cars, sports bikes and encroached ashrams."

He had had similar conversations before with Javed and he knew what Javed would say. He would point to people like Ambedkar who had done just that: take an ancient religion and use a reformed version of it to tell the world how society should look like. So maybe Javed was right to be doing what he did. After all, a world that can ignore Ambedkar surely wouldn't listen to Javed. He realised there was no point in bugging Javed. He was doing what he should be doing.

He was done bargaining with Javed and was happy to reach acceptance. Maybe this acceptance was adulthood: understanding that things won't be as you think they should; and exploiting the way things are for personal profit.

After the call ended with long-drawn out goodbyes, Alice saw that he had a couple of missed calls from Chikki. He called her back.

'Hi. Busy?'

'No. Want to hang out?' asked Chikki immediately.

'Yeah. Get some Old Monk. I am in a blah mood but also a blah-blah mood. Be prepared to do some serious listening.'

'Done. Send me some money.' Drinking at Alice's meant AC in the living room. So Chikki was always ready.

'Yeah. Pick up mixers and snacks too.'

Chikki landed at Alice's in no more than half an hour, arms bursting with bottles and packets of food. Alice knew that the next few months would be tough. He would have to seriously try to figure out what he wanted out of life. They brought glasses out from the kitchen and arranged the food and drinks on the coffee table with care. Alice poured them both a glass of rum and cola and squeezed a lemon wedge into both their drinks. He decided to remain in the shattered remnants of the bubble for one more evening before returning to reality.

'In college, we always bottoms upped the first drink,' Alice said, raising his glass.

Chikki grinned broadly and raised her glass. 'Can you still do it?'

'I'll regret it tomorrow, but right now, I can!' Alice cheers-ed and chugged his drink, coughing and gagging a couple of times.

Chikki laughed and finished her drink effortlessly, cleaned the table with a cloth and poured them both another drink. 'So, what do you want to talk about?' asked Chikki, leaning in conspiratorially.

'I am starting a cult. Can I count on you to be my first apostle?'

'Cult? Yeah. I can do cult. But what's it about? It's not a suicide cult, no?' Chikki asked with a raised eyebrow.

'No, no. Suicide takes too much commitment. We'll actually be reviving an ancient extinct religion,' explained Alice. 'And the pitch goes something like this: We are all trapped in a thought matrix that imprisons our minds and actions. The Ajivika religion frees our minds and expands our consciousness and stuff like that.'

'That's it?' asked Chikki suspiciously.

'Yeah. That's pretty much it. The long and short of it. I mean there's other things like being silent and non-judgemental. You'll figure it out by and by.'

'Cool, yeah. It's short and sweet,' said Chikki, grinning widely. 'I am so happy you picked me to be your first disciple.'

'Apostle. And are you kidding? Of course I pick you. You are the rock upon which I will build my church.'

'There's a church?' asked Chikki.

'Yeah,' replied Alice. 'The triple platinum church of Neo-Ajivikism.' Alice made a mental note to excavate his cupboard for his diary. Apart from Javed's aphorisms it had a lot of other content that could help. He hadn't written in it for years. He felt like it was a good time to start again.

'Hardcore. I am so sold on this. What do I have to do?' asked Chikki, interrupting his thoughts.

Alice furrowed his brows and looked away wistfully. 'Record the story of how the church was established. But through my eyes.' What if he didn't have a partner to stand testimony to his life and times? He had an apostle.

'Cool. When do we start?' asked Chikki, rapidly clapping her hands.

'Right now.' Alice sipped his drink. He set the glass on the table and interlocked his fingers. 'It was winter in Delhi. I was sleeping all wrapped up in a blanket when I had this crazy dream…'

ABOUT THE AUTHOR

Satwik Gade is an illustrator and writer based in Chennai. His work has been featured in *The Hindu*, *Firstpost*, *BuzzFeed*, and other news and lifestyle portals. He illustrates children's books for Karadi Tales, Tulika Books and BLPS.

30 Years *of*

 HarperCollins *Publishers* India

At HarperCollins, we believe in telling the best stories and finding the widest possible readership for our books in every format possible. We started publishing 30 years ago; a great deal has changed since then, but what has remained constant is the passion with which our authors write their books, the love with which readers receive them, and the sheer joy and excitement that we as publishers feel in being a part of the publishing process.

Over the years, we've had the pleasure of publishing some of the finest writing from the subcontinent and around the world, and some of the biggest bestsellers in India's publishing history. Our books and authors have won a phenomenal range of awards, and we ourselves have been named Publisher of the Year the greatest number of times. But nothing has meant more to us than the fact that millions of people have read the books we published, and somewhere, a book of ours might have made a difference.

As we step into our fourth decade, we go back to that one word – a word which has been a driving force for us all these years.

Read.

Harper
Collins

HARPER
PERENNIAL

HARPER
BUSINESS

HARPER
BLACK

हार्पर
हिन्दी

HarperCollins
Children'sBooks

HARPER
DESIGN

HARPER
VANTAGE

Harper
Sport